# The Visitor &

# Other Threesomes:

## Friendly MMF Ménage Tales

### K. D. West

Stillpoint/Eros

## Print ISBN: 978-1-938808-26-5
## Ebook ISBN: 978-1-938808-25-8

*Erotica to feed the mind, the spirit…
and, oh, yes, the body.
Fine erotica for the discerning individual,
available as ebooks, print books, and audiobooks!*

StillpointEros.com

# Stillpoint/Eros
STILLNESS AND ECSTASY...

## K.D. West's Friendly Ménage Tales

### Collections:

*The Visitor and Other Threesomes*[†] (FMM)
*The Visitor Arrives: A Quartet of Friendly Ménage Tales*[*†] (FMM)
*Three for Three: A Trio of Friendly MMF Ménage Tales... Plus!*[†] (MMF, FMM, MFM)

### Stories:

*The Visitor*[*] (FMM)
*The Visitor Comes Home*[*] (FMM)
*The Visitor Comes Again*[*] (FMM)
*The Visitor Goes to Work*[*] (FMM)
*The Visitor Entertains* (FMM - coming soon!)
*The Visitor Takes a Trip* (FMM - coming soon!)
*The Visitor Has Company* (FMM, FFM - coming soon!)

*Truth & Games*[*] (FMM)
*Over the Top*[*] (MFM, MF)
*Folding Herself In* (MFM)

*Juliet Takes the Floor*[*] (MF, FF - Now available!)
*Juliet Takes Charge* (MF, FF, FFM - Coming soon!)
*Juliet Takes Flight* (MF, FF, FFM - Coming soon!)

*Opening the Door* (MFF - Coming soon!)
*The Trouble with Triplets* (MMF, MFF - Coming soon!)

[*] *Available now as an audiobook on Audible, iTunes, Amazon & Stillpoint/Eros. All titles will be available soon!*
[†] *Available now in print from Amazon, Barnes & Noble, Stillpoint/Eros & other fine booksellers*

FMM = *A woman with two men, from the woman's point of view*
MMF = *A man with a man and woman from the man's point of view*
MFM = *A woman with two men; no sexual contact between the men*
FFM = *A woman with a man and woman from the woman's point of view*
MFF = *A man with two women from the man's point of view*

# Contents

# The Visitor Arrives

## A girl, her fireman...
## and her other fireman

# The Visitor

Lea didn't usually masturbate in airplane bathrooms, because, after all, they're bathrooms. On airplanes.

But half of the way through the long flight across the country to Atlanta, she found herself in the tiny, tinny cubicle with one foot up on the wall and the other in the sink, with her fingers buried to the second knuckle in her pussy.

Thinking of Sean, her best friend's older brother.

Sean the firefighter of the broad shoulders and the narrow hips. Sean of the gentle Southern drawl, the polite tone, the blue eyes, and the wicked, square-jawed smile.

Sean, who she had always wanted to wrap her arms and legs around, but never managed to do more than flirt with a bit.

Sean. Who had found out that she was interviewing for the job in Atlanta and had, with smooth, apparently subtext-less Southern hospitality, invited her to save the cost of a hotel room and stay with him. Well, on the sofa of the apartment he shared. But still. Just a door away... *Oooo, Sean.*

She wanted him. She had always wanted him, since she was a college sophomore and his sister Kirsten's roomie. She wanted his strong arms around her. Wanted his big hands pulling her pelvis *tight* against his. Wanted to feel what she knew would be his big, thick cock spreading... *Ooo...!*

With a shudder of pleasure and relief that she knew was only temporary, she came, swallowing as best she could the groan that wanted to explode from her gut.

Carefully, quickly, Lea lowered her legs, pulled up her panties, pulled down her skirt and smoothed it as best she could, washed her hands, and opened the bathroom door.

A woman just a few years older than Lea stood in the narrow galley glaring daggers at her. Her elbow-high child was doing a dance that made unmistakably clear just how long they'd had to wait.

"Sorry," Lea murmured. "Thanks."

"Yaw're welcome," the mother grumbled in a thick-as-honey accent that made Lea feel anything but welcome as the woman and her child pushed past.

Even so, hearing that Southern sound got Lea thinking of Sean again, of his arms and chest and ass and mouth... and got her wondering just how long the mom and kid were going to take, because, *oh*, she could have started all over, airplane bathroom or no.

•••

The plane finally landed and Lea picked up the beat-up old Civic she'd rented. Sean had told her that he'd have loved to pick her up, but he wasn't going to be getting off duty until about the time Lea landed, and since she was going to need a car the next day anyway to get to the interview, she drove herself north from the airport — around the city and into Cobb County, where Sean and the other firefighter shared a place, where she'd be sleeping on their couch.

*Well,* she thought, *let's not lie*: Lea hoped that she *wouldn't* be sleeping on their couch. She hoped very much that she would at last be sharing Sean's bed. She knew that she should have been thinking about the interview, but hey — there are lots of jobs. There was only one Sean, and she'd lusted after him for far too long.

*Well.*

She *was* thinking about the job interview. It was for the position of assistant business manager of a mid-sized professional theater — her chance finally to work somewhere other than the glorified community theaters she'd been slaving at since graduation. She was excited by the opportunity.

*But Sean....*

Her thoughts less on the road than they should have been, she followed her phone's directions around the city, past dozens of malls, hotels, and office buildings mostly bearing the name *Peachtree Whatever,* and out into the gently rolling hills and lush greenery of the Atlanta suburbs.

"Exit the highway," said her phone, and she exited. "Turn left," it intoned, and she turned left.

She wondered if she could give her GPS voice a Southern accent. *Tuhn leyeft, honey.* That thought made Lea smile.

She reached the complex, parked, and followed Sean's very clear directions to his second-floor apartment. Fighting down the images of Sean's broad chest — and narrow hips — that had driven her to the airplane lavatory, she knocked on the door.

A muffled voice called out, "C'me in! It's unlocked."

She opened the door and was assaulted simultaneously by the delicious smells of something sweet baking and something frying, as well as by the vision of the tall, tapered figure at the stove.

*Him.* Cooking. Looking like every masturbatory fantasy Lea had ever had about him, only better. Except fully dressed, but *food. Shit.*

"Sorry I couldn't come to the door," he said in that sweet Georgia drawl. He finished flipping something in the pan. "I'm up to my elbows in fried chicken. Hope you like — "

Lea threw her arms around him from behind and took joy in squeezing his chest hard. "I love it! Thank you so much for having me."

"Uh. Welcome." He stiffened before relaxing and turning in her grasp. "Nice to meet you, too, miss."

Lea looked up at the eyes smiling down at her. Brown. At the dimpled chin. *Not Sean. Oh, SHIT.* She released the man — he had to be Sean's roomie — and stammered, "I'm so, so... I, uh..."

"Naw, miss, don't be sorry, that was a nice hello, no doubt!" The roommate put down his tongs and smiled at her. He held out his enormous hand. "I'm Andrew. You must be Lea."

She shook his hand and nodded, still speechless.

His grin grew. "Really, don't feel bad. It happens more often than you'd think — the captain mixes us up so much he's taken to just calling us the Twins."

"Huh," Lea grunted. She was feeling the ghost of that muscled chest on her fingers.

"There you are, Lea!" Another Southern voice called from the other side of the apartment. She turned: it was Sean, no doubt this time. Blue eyes. Square jaw. Nothing on but a towel around his waist. *Oh. Shitty shit-shit.* He ran his hand through his short, wet hair. "Sorry, I was just taking a shower, I didn't want you to have to smell me like the hog I am."

"Huh," Lea repeated.

Sean smiled warmly. "I see you met Andy. I hope, Andy," he said, his voice lowering in mock threat, "that you've conducted yourself like a gentleman toward this young lady."

"I wasn't the one came out half-naked," joked Andy.

Lea found her voice. "Besides, I was the one molesting *him.*"

Sean raised his eyebrow, that supremely wicked grin on display.

"Yeah," laughed Andy, "lucky me! She thought I was *you*. Couldn't see your ugly face 'cause I was dealing with supper."

"*My* ugly face!"

"Anyhow," Andy laughed, "why didn't you tell me our visitor was such a bombshell? Begging your pardon, Miss Lea."

Lea felt Sean's eyes flash to hers, saw the smile turn from wicked to evil. "Didn't want you getting ideas, Andy."

Lea couldn't think of anything to say to that.

"Ideas, huh?" Andy snorted and turned back to the stove. "You go get some pants on, boy, and we'll have some supper and then we can talk about who's getting *ideas*."

Now Sean's grin turned sunny again; he waved and turned, and Lea was treated to the sight of his retreating, naked, rippling back and his tight, towel-clad ass as they made their way down the hall.

*I'm getting ideas*, Lea thought, and then tried very hard not to think any more.

• • •

Dinner — *supper* — was of course fried chicken, with, of course, corn on the cob and amazing peach pie. "You've now hit all of the high points of Georgia cuisine," Sean joked.

"Hey!" said Andy, "we haven't even got to grits and boiled peanuts!"

Making a face, Sean said, "What a shame."

"You call yourself a Georgia boy?" said Andy. "You're all city, Sean, admit it."

"You have to be from the country to be a Georgian?" Sean raised an eyebrow.

"Naturally," Andy replied. "Q.E.D."

Trying not to get totally lost in enjoying their banter (*flirtation?*), Lea said, "Sounds like something my mom always used to say: if you live in New York, you're Jewish. If you're Jewish living outside New York, you're *goyisch*. Um, gentile."

"Me," said Sean, "I have always considered myself a citizen of the world."

Andy laughed, "Yeah, listen to the cosmopolitan here. Visit's his sister off in California, and he comes back talking about *artichokes* and pizza with all kinds of fancy stuff on it, and *sushi*."

"I didn't know you liked sushi, Sean!" To be honest, Lea couldn't remember Sean ever eating a meal that he didn't seem to enjoy.

"Oh," Sean said, he eyes holding hers once more, "I *love* sushi." His tone barely changed, and his expression seemed to hold exactly the same open, welcoming grin, but there was something about the way he said it that made Lea's middle flutter as she imagined him kneeling between her legs. Imagined the feeling of his tongue... He winked.

He's flirting with me, Lea reveled. Oh, god, yes, he's flirting with me.

Andy laughed again and popped open another beer for Lea. "Now see, *me*, I like my fish too, but I like it as the first course, not the main dish."

Lea's eyes snapped to Andy's and she saw that he too had a lazy, sexy smile on, and that — yes — she hadn't imagined the sexual undertones this time either. *Playing games, gentlemen?* She took a swig of her cold beer and twirled the drumstick bone she'd been fiddling with. "Well," she said, letting her voice grow raspy, "I like my meat red, generally. Love to chew on a rib, for instance. Nice, long, hard rib, dripping juices down my chin..." She ran her tongue up the length of the bone. "*Mmm.*" When both men's jaws dropped, she couldn't help it: she laughed.

Sean and Andy were both turning bright red, but they too laughed, long and hard.

"Mind," Lea finally managed to say, waving the bone, "this chicken really was fabulous."

"Thank you," Andy said with a smile and mock bow.

They proceeded to drink and talk. And drink some more. Beer. And then some bourbon. And then some more.

And Lea was flirting with two fantastically hot firemen, and they were both flirting back, and she felt absolutely fucking fabulous.

And just at the point that Lea was ready to pull her shirt off and yell, *COME TO MAMA!* to them both, Sean — or maybe it was Andy — stood up and reminded Lea that she had an interview in the morning. And then Andy — or maybe it was Sean — walked remarkably steadily over to the couch, pulled it out, and began to make up Lea's bed.

And the other helped.

For a brief moment, watching the two burly boys arranging her pillows and smoothing her sheets with an almost military precision, Lea indulged in an image of both of them stripping off their t-shirts, dropping their jeans and joining her....

But then both stepped away, wished her a good night, and sauntered together back toward where their bedrooms were. Each seemed to be trying to make sure that the other was leaving the room first, but eventually they left side by side, their shoulders barely clearing the hallway walls.

Well, shit.

As Lea slipped off her skirt, her shirt, her bra, and the panties that she'd been wanting to shed since she entered the apartment, she stood there, horny, naked, and more than a little drunk. *I could sneak into Sean's bed,* she thought. *He wouldn't kick me out, I know it. Or Andy's. Or...*

She shook her head. No. They'd made the sensible choice. She sat down and started to look for her pajamas....

But the air was warm and thick.

And she was tired. And light-headed.

And so she slipped, pajama-less, under the covers in the fold-out bed, dreaming that the fingers stroking her clit and teasing her nipples belonged to two very large, very strong, very different sets of hands.

•••

Lea's dream was very, very pleasant. In it, someone… Or perhaps more than one someone… Well. In either case, licking of her foot was involved, by a tongue or tongues unknown. *Mmm.*

Her eyes fluttered open.

It wasn't a dream.

A tongue was in fact running up Lea's instep, sending a flare to her crotch that caused her to writhe on her belly and groan. *Mmm.*

"Hey, Lea." The voice was soft and male and Southern. "Thought you might want some company."

Between the pleasant suddenness of her wakening and the alcohol that was still in her system, Lea could only manage a throaty "Uh-huh." She spread her legs wide, her foot pulling the sheet aside and uncovering her lower body.

"Mmm," whispered the voice. "I like peach pie just fine, but this was what I wanted for dessert."

"Uh… *huh!*"

Without warning the tongue had slid all of the way up her inner thigh and licked the entire length of her pussy, sending Lea's smoldering arousal into full flame.

"Shh." He chuckled. "Don't want to wake no one. 'Cept you, 'course."

Lea wanted to say something smart, but a whimper was the best she could do. Her pelvis arched up of its own accord.

Whichever of the men he was, he was clearly a gentleman. He took the invitation graciously and dove in. His tongue and lips began to tease and pleasure her lips and clit. His nose tickled her asshole, the hot breath sending what was already an indescribable sensation truly transcendent.

"Hnnnh!"

"Shh," he said again, this time against her clit.

Trembling, Lea stuffed her face into the pillow, screaming into it as he pleasured her with his tongue, his lips, his nose. When his fingers slid up under her belly and began to massage her breasts, she lost all sense of what was happening and where — her body was one nerve, pulsing, *now.*

Usually, Lea liked long, slow bouts of foreplay, liked kissing and touching and feeling a man slowly meander his way to going down on her. There was something wonderfully romantic about watching a head wandering down her belly and between her thighs. Nose bobbing as he lapped at her. Eyes open and smoldering or closed and abandoned as he pleasured her.

But this? Having her face shoved into the pillow, her ass up in the air, and that *mouth.* . . . Even if Lea had been on her back, even if it had been less than pitch black, she didn't think that she'd have been able to see straight anyway.

Thick, strong fingers pulled and teased remarkably gently at her nipples, causing her to scream on into the pillow as wide, fine lips sucked her sizzling clit against a fluttering tongue. *Cleft chin, or square?* she found herself wondering for a moment, though of course his chin was down between her spread thighs where she couldn't tell. But then an electric spark began to shoot from her clit up her spine, joining with the arcs of pleasure fired by those amazing fingers in flaring up to her brain and shutting down all thought quite effectively.

Thunder rumbled. At first, Lea thought it was her imagination, part of the monumental orgasm that set her aflame. Then, as the explosion subsided, she realized that not all of the lightning was inside of her. There was a storm outside, the kind that rarely visited Lea's home state.

Her visitor was kissing his way from her right cheek of her ass across the dimple at the base of her spine to the left cheek.

"Fuck me," moaned Lea into the pillow. "*Fuckmefuckme.*"

"Yes, ma'am," said the deep voice. "Always give a lady what she asks for, that's what I was always taught." She heard him fishing for something, heard the distinctive crinkle of a foil condom package being opened, a rubber being rolled down over a hard cock. A wide hand ran over her ass, her back, sending a tremor through Lea. . "Like this, or — ?"

*"Fuck. Me."* She reached back between her legs, found a hard, long, latex-encased penis, and pulled it toward her.

"Yes, ma'am," he said, a quaver of desire in his voice that made Lea feel incredibly sexy and incredibly hot and that made her want him inside of her *right now.*

Again: Lea usually preferred to face her lover — whether in straight missionary position or with a leg or two over his shoulders — for a couple of reasons. First of all, she liked being able to see the affect she had on a man, could be in itself an incredible turn on. Second, she liked the feeling of the cock plowing the front wall of her pussy. Lea had discovered her G-spot long before she'd ever heard the term, had discovered that, unlike most of her girlfriends, she could have a very satisfying orgasm just from being fucked (so long as her lover was big enough and lasted long enough).

Just now, however, she didn't mind being banged from behind, her face still stuffed into her pillow.

As this cock head pressed into Lea's pussy, however, she gasped in surprise, feeling it surge along the front wall of her vagina: this cock, unlike any she'd ever had inside of her, curved *down.*

It was perfect.

It made her *scream.* If there was thunder and lightning rolling on, Lea couldn't have seen or heard, because the cock that was now pounding hard into her sent her nerves roaring, her blood screaming.

Orgasm, which hadn't ever quite left her, came howling back, playing hide-and-seek with her consciousness as her visitor slammed into her, one massive paw pulling her hips back against him as the other reached around and found...

Found her clit, and...

*Oh, FUCK.*

• • •

Was she dreaming again? Was it all just one enormous, wet blurry wet....

Lea's fingers reached down her belly between her legs. No cock. No cock, but fabulously tender. Wet.

Had she hallucinated it? Or had she passed out, drunk and spent on whiskey and sex?

Blearily she turned over, looking for...

Lightning flashed, revealing a broad-shouldered silhouette. "Fuck," he said. "You are so fucking beautiful."

*So are you*, Lea tried to say, but couldn't be sure that any intelligible sound had passed her lips. She reached up, her slick fingers finding a muscled chest, caressing a tiny, jewel-hard nipple.

"*Shit.*" He hissed, and leaned forward, his lips finding hers as the retreating storm finally rumbled its own approval.

The flame inside of Lea, barely banked, flared back to light. Not quite so urgent as before, but no less strong, and so she pulled his body to hers, burying herself in him, running her finger along his ribs, the muscles of his back, feeling that hard cock, un-rubbered now, straining and leaking against the outside of her thigh.

Yet he seemed in no hurry this time, and so Lea was able to indulge and kiss and explore.

Her fingers counted the vertebrae down to the taut swell of his ass, the concave plane of his hips.

His fingers flowed slowly, reverentially over her flesh: her hips, her belly.

*Down? Please?*

Well, no: as they kissed, as their tongues danced, those amazing, enormous, shockingly *delicate* fingers explored upward, skirting the outside of one aching breast, defining the line of her collar bone, of her throat, her earlobe....

How was it that a light touch against her ear could make goose pimples erupt all of the way down to her knees? She moaned into his mouth; desire clutched her again, throbbing through her. She wanted him inside of her — wanted him *so much* — and yet...

And yet the passion of their last fuck and the languor of this session had left her without will, without a muscle in her body. She was his, to take at whatever pace it pleased him, and *oooohhh*, it pleased him to take his sweet, sweet, Georgia-peach time, and it pleased her to be taken so.

Lea had lost her virginity during the summer before her senior year of high school. She and Sam had been dating for two years at that point, and had done just about everything that could be done with fingers and mouths, and so Lea hadn't been shocked at Sam's urgency or his hair trigger. Not shocked, but disappointed. They'd eventually worked out how to make sure that she got her fair share out of their sessions: it had usually involved lots of kissing and caressing, ending with his head between her thighs. He hadn't been exactly patient, but he had at least tried, the sweetie.

Of the dozen or so lovers she'd had since, the more successful had usually followed a similar formula: petting her until she was worked up, getting her off with their tongues, then pumping into her until *they* got off. When she was really lucky, the man lasted long enough and was properly endowed — neither too well nor not well enough — so that the pressure of his cock against her G-spot and his pelvis against her clit got her off again before he exploded.

None of them had ever managed to set her alight without actually touching her crotch.

Her new lover was getting dangerously close. All with a slow, gentle touch that spread over her like honey on fire.

He broke their kiss, and Lea whimpered. And yet when the lips began a voyage along her chin to her ear, tongue flowing lightly around the lobe and *in* before continuing down her neck even as those amazing fingers began to outline the curves of her breasts, she found that she couldn't complain.

He kissed on down, licking at the hollow of her throat and at her chest, at the top of one swelling, aching breast, even as his fingers traced the bottom of her rib cage, the lines of the abs she never thought she had, the tightly trimmed bush of her pubes.

And at the same bright, shining moment, his lips closed around her right nipple as one of his hands caressed the other and the other hand slid over her pussy lips, stroking her vibrating clit.

Even in the moment, Lea was disappointed that she couldn't have enjoyed that slow, fabulous journey for longer. Even in the moment, Lea knew that she felt so fucking *good*.

Clenching her jaw, pressing her mouth against the top of his head, she screamed once again, her thighs clamping around his hand as a slow-motion tidal wave of an orgasm sloshed up through her and back down, leaving her limp and quivering.

She collapsed, her head flopping back, her legs falling apart, her eyes falling closed and her mouth falling wide open.

*Holy fucking shit. Fuck. Oh, fuck.*

How long had they been at it? Ten minutes? An hour? Long enough for the storm to have wandered away. Long enough for her to have come three times, each as hard as she could ever remember coming. *And I don't even know which…*

He kissed her breast lightly, his fingers still on the other nipple, his other hand still gently cupping her pussy. "God," he groaned, "you're so fucking *wet*."

"For *you*," she rasped. "You… fuck? *Please*."

"Oh, God, *yes*," he hissed, and Lea once again heard the sound of a hand fumbling in a pocket, of a foil packet being ripped.

This time she wanted to help roll the latex down over that magnificent erection, but her arms were boneless. She heard him grunt as he finished putting on the condom — next time, she'd have to invest in an IUD or a diaphragm or any fucking thing so they wouldn't have to *wait*….

Lea started to roll on her belly again, but he stopped her. "Naw," he sighed. "Wanna see you."

And so, half-conscious, she lay back as he slid between her legs, placing himself at her entrance. "Ready?" he grunted.

Lea nodded, or thought she did.

Whichever, he pressed himself in, filling Lea with airless, dark flame. "*Fuck!*"

"Yup." Lea grinned. Felt her entire body grin.

As he slowly pressed in, stretching her wide once again, he leaned down and kissed her — no teasing this time, just lips on lips. Closing the circuit.

In close embrace, in full contact from nose to knee, they began to fuck. *Fuck indeed!*

Well, to be completely honest, she was still as limp as a rag doll. He was doing the fucking, slowly, with agonizing tenderness that was just as intoxicating as the wild abandon from earlier. She could feel flare of his cock pressing along the ripples of her vaginal walls, could feel...

*Fuck.*

As they fucked — as he fucked her — his hands continued to explore, to enrapture. She could feel him stoking the flickering flame of her arousal, could feel it building, but so, so slowly that it made her want to weep, even as it made her want to sing.

John, with whom she'd lived for almost a year before moving back in with Kirsten, had gotten off on tying Lea up, teasing her. *Edging*, he called it: keeping her on the verge of coming for as long as he could before finally giving her release — but only when she was begging for it.

She'd gone along with this game because it felt fucking *good*, but it had turned out to be one of a number of clues that he was a controlling asshole. A pleasant clue, but still.

This slow, slow fuck didn't feel like Lea's lover was trying to control her. It simply felt as if he was *in control*, savoring the delight with her, as if they were sharing a particularly fabulous meal.

"You... feel so fucking... *good*," he moaned into Lea's mouth.

Once again, "Yup" was all that Lea could reply. Or possibly "Yum."

She could feel a slick layer of sweat beginning to form between them, could feel his nipples, small and tight, dragging against hers, could feel the blood build up around her G-spot as the fabulous, wonderful, unbelievable cock massaged it, gently but mercilessly. Could feel arousal expanding her infinitely outward

"*Legs*," she panted, "*up....*"

He understood, apparently, because he slid his hands down under her knees and lifted them as he arched backward and pressed her calves upward with his square shoulders. Opening her to him. All without stopping his thrusts.

The change in angle absolutely scrambled what was left of Lea's brain, as her body clearly had clearly known that it would. The fuck was the only thing that existed in the world. It was a universal fuck. A metaphysical fuck.

He was speeding up — minutely, but noticeably, he pistoned into her more quickly, more forcefully. Lea wanted to beg him not to come too soon, to wait for the avalanche that was bearing down on her to sweep her away.

But her lips wouldn't form words.

His thrusts began to become less and less measured, more and more frantic, and Lea almost wept, because it felt so *fucking good*, but she was *so close* and...

And as her demon lover gave one last gigantic, spastic thrust, he reached between them and pushed his wide thumb firmly but gently against her clit, pressing it against the base of his cock, and...

And the avalanche carried her off in a flood of white pleasure, and if she were never to wake again, she considered it a fair trade. *Aloha. Shalom. Arrivaderci. Sayonara.*

• • •

To her surprise, however, she didn't die.

"Oh, gawd, oh, gawd," her lover gasped, his chest heaving against hers. Her legs were bent nearly flat against her torso, a level of flexibility she'd never quite managed in yoga, but was reveling in now, because she could *feel* his cock still within her, still pulsing. Which caused her to contract around him. Which made them both call out to a higher power.

Carefully, still buried in her, he released her legs. With as much regret as relief — more — she lowered them, squeezing his softening erection out of her body, which made both of them moan at the loss.

Lea became aware that her back, her ass, her legs — they were all burning. She was going to be sore as all fuck the next day.

But it was worth it.

They lay there, still entangled, as their breaths and pulses slowed. They kissed again.

No frenzy. Just touching.

She must have fallen asleep at some point, because she startled to find him tucking her under the covers.

"Shh," he said, and placed a feather-light kiss on her forehead. "You get some sleep, now, you hear?"

"'Night," she rasped.

But he was gone.

One last distant rumble of thunder shook the night.

And all was darkness.

• • •

When Lea's phone started crowing at her to wake up and greet the bright new day while the sky was still dark — while it was still the middle of the night back on the West Coast — she slapped at it with a groan. *Fucking...*

Fucking.

*Thunder. And a mouth on my foot. And a nose against my asshole. And a cock screwing me into the pillow. Fingers like feathers of fire. A slow, full-body fuck for the ages.*

*Fucking...*

**Must** *have been a dream, right?*

Lea shifted, trying to shake the cobwebs from her brain, and her body screamed at her that it had been no dream. She was sore from knees to nose, but it was a fabulous sore, not like anything she'd ever endured after a run or a yoga class.

Trying to sort out just what had happened from the swirling mass of over-amped sensory impressions, Lea rolled (somewhat tenderly) to the side of the pull-out mattress.

*Amazing you're still standing.* She patted the sofa-sleeper on the arm-rest. *Well done!*

Grabbing toiletries and her bathrobe, she made her way to the bathroom.

Which was right between the two firemen's bedrooms.

*Which one was it?* She couldn't decide whether she wanted her phantom lover to have been the man she'd had a crush on since she was nineteen or the stranger she'd just met.

Either way, they were both snoring, clearly sound asleep.

One of them had truly earned it, that was for sure.

Smiling — still moving gingerly — she went into the bathroom, closed the door somewhat regretfully, and took a long, hot shower that almost returned her body to her.

When she wrapped herself in her robe and stepped out of the steamy bathroom, she was greeted by two very solemn looking, bare-chested boys.

"Morning, Miss Lea," Andy said, while Sean simply turned "Lea" into an eight-syllable twelve-bar-blues of a mumble.

"Good morning, gentlemen!" she chirped, thinking, *One of you was the best fuck I have ever had in my life, and I have no idea which of you it was.*

"What do y'all want for breakfast?" mumbled Andy.

Sean muttered back, "You made supper, Andy. I'll take care of this one."

Each of them had his eyes on her, but even so, both of them seemed more aware of each other than of her.

*Oh, god,* she groaned inwardly, *they're both trying to mark their territory.* And while the idea held a certain amount of abstract fascination, she had absolutely no interest in being fought over or peed on. "It seems to me, gentlemen," she said, aiming for sweet-and-unassailable, "that it's your day off, and you've already provided me with a lovely meal and a lovely bed." She looked to see if either of them took that any way but literally, but their expressions remained stony. "It would be my pleasure to cook breakfast. *Y'all* go sit, and I'll cook."

When they tried to object, she reached out and grabbed each by the chest hair, twisting just enough to get their attention.

Their eyes bugged out and their jaws dropped, but they consented to sit together at the table.

Lea chatted away, pulling eggs and sausages out of the fridge — remarkably clean for a pair of guys, but hey, firemen know about hygiene, right? She had the sausages frying and was whipping the eggs when the sun broke through the clouds that were the only evidence of the previous night's storm. "Man," she sighed, taking in the golden light that washed over the small woods behind the apartment, feeling the warmth on her gloriously weary body, "will you look at that. Just gorgeous."

She hadn't really said it for their benefit, and so she hadn't *really* expected them to answer, but still, she was surprised when all she heard from behind her was a quiet choking sound.

Both of them were staring at her, jaws dropped, eyes wide.

*Oh. Fuck. Silk robe.* She started to try to make her silhouette a bit more modest, but then thought, *What the fuck, why not?* Standing there, knowing that they could see the outline of her body very clearly, she repeated. "Gorgeous. Don't you think?"

"Yes, ma'am," they both answered, making Lea laugh.

As the sausage sizzled away in the pan and the eggs cooked, she thought, *Look as much as you want, gentlemen. One of you owns all of this already.* And then a thought occurred to her that made her blush and grin: *And if I can figure out who it was, maybe I'll give all of it to the other one tonight!*

When she brought the breakfast to the table, both men kept their eyes glued to their food.

*More's the pity,* sighed Lea, as they ate in silence.

When they were done, Lea started to clear, but Sean stopped her. "Naw, you cooked, we'll clean."

"You should get ready for your interview," said Andy, very seriously.

And so Lea left them to it, grabbing her garment bag and retreating back to the bathroom.

In the bathroom, she took stock. *No more thinking about hunky firefighters,* she scolded herself. *Time to go get yourself a job.*

When she came out, hair tamed (more or less), makeup sparingly applied, battle armor on, ready to take on the world, the two men were still in the kitchen, which was indeed now clean. They still didn't seem to have anything to say to each other. They were standing, arms crossed, leaning against the counter.

"You look lovely, Lea," said Sean, which made her middle go soft.

"Gorgeous," added Andy, making it go warm.

"Thanks, boys." She took a deep breath, trying to focus on the interview, and not on their muscular torsos. "Wish me luck."

"Good luck," they said in unison, and away she went.

The interview went far better than Lea had even hoped. She hit it off immediately with the business manager, a sardonic, middle-aged Canadian with the unlikely name of Sassy ("It's Sally actually, but they started calling me Saskatchewan, which they then shortened, and it's kind of stuck.") By late morning, they were swapping war stories, and Sassy dragged Lea out of her office to show her through the entire building, introducing Lea to staff as they went — an army of fundraisers, marketers, and box office staff, then backstage to meet technicians and the wardrobe department, and finally into a rehearsal — a set designer was showing the cast what the stage was going to look like, so it must have been a read-through. When the cast took an Equity break, Sassy buttonholed Bob, the artistic director of the theater, and asked him to join her and Lea for a late lunch at the barbecue joint across the street.

Trying not to think too much about the fact that she was now having lunch with the senior management of a theater that Lea would kill to work at, she gnawed away at her pork ribs.

"I think this is how we keep Sassy here," said Bob with a broad smile.

"It's true," said Sassy, smirking. "Every time I want to head back to the great white north, someone drops a take-out bag of ribs on my desk, and I know I can't leave."

"We have our ways," Bob chuckled.

As they bantered on, Lea felt the sauce from the rib she was chewing on dribbling onto her chin, and she couldn't help but remember teasing Sean and Andy with just that image the previous night, couldn't help but remember their stunned expressions.

Couldn't help but remember what happened after the lights went out.

"Well, something's got you smiling," Sassy said.

"It's the barbecue," said Lea as she dabbed at her chin. "I can see why you can't leave it behind."

They all laughed.

They offered her the job before she'd even finished eating, and she accepted on the spot. The pay wasn't great, and she'd have to leave California and her best friend, but the opportunity was too good to pass up.

"Are you going to need help finding a place to stay?" asked Sassy, clearing their sauce-soaked baskets.

"I... think I may have one lined up." This brought an even broader grin to Lea's face than before.

She called back to the apartment. One of them — she thought it was Andy — picked up, and before he could say more than "Hello," she shouted, "I got the job! Dinner tonight's on me!"

"Well, congratulations!" said whichever of the men was on the phone.

And before he could say anything more, she hung up and did a dance, right there in the restaurant.

• • •

When she walked back up the stairs to the apartment a couple of hours later, she had in one hand an enormous bag full of barbecue chicken from the same joint she'd had lunch at, with orders of fried okra and corn bread. In the other hand, she swung a bottle of Maker's Mark, with which she knocked against the door.

Just like the day before, a muffled voice called out, "C'me in! It's unlocked."

"Can't!" she called back. "Hands full!"

"Hold on," said a slightly closer voice, and the door swung open, revealing Sean, who was still wearing nothing but low-slung pajama bottoms.

Andy was sitting at the kitchen table, identically dressed.

"Haven't you guys even gotten dressed all day?" Lea laughed and gave Sean a sound kiss on the lips.

He looked astonished, but Andy scowled.

"None of that!" burbled Lea, dancing into the kitchen and giving him an equally sound smooch. That seemed to cheer him up. "Tonight, we're celebrating!" She held up the barbecue and the bourbon.

They were happy to go along with this plan, and were soon all stuffed and pleasantly buzzed. Between the warmth, the Southern humidity, the food, and the alcohol, Lea was getting sweaty, but she couldn't have cared less. She was hoping to get a whole lot sweatier. *Now which of you was my mystery man last night*, she found herself wondering as she took off her jacket and tossed it in the general direction of the pullout. *And am I going to get him to fuck me again, or am I going to try out the other one. Or...*

She looked back at the two men, whiskey-wild thoughts bouncing through her head.

They were both staring at her. At her chest. Both licking their lips.

When she looked down, she saw that sweat had made her white silk blouse all but translucent. The lace bra showed clearly through. She grinned at them. "Well, gentlemen, like what you see?"

They both looked back up at her, hunger and shock plain on their faces.

Lea stood and walked around to their side of the table, unbuttoning her blouse as she went. "I have a confession to make, guys."

"Oh?" said Sean with a gulp, his eyes following her fingers' journey down from button to button.

Andy's eyes were still on Lea's tits.

"Uh-huh. I had a visitor in my bed last night."

Both men turned bright red and looked down at their feet.

*Aha! Gotcha!* "I got fucked good. And hard. And long."

They both gulped.

"Now, it was dark last night, and so I couldn't see just who this mystery lover was, and so all today, I've been trying to figure out." She knelt between them. "Was it you, Andy?" She touched him on the knee and tried not to laugh when he jumped. "Or you, Sean?" She ran her fingers up the inside of his thigh and he let out a choking sound.

"And as we were eating that wonderful barbecue tonight, I've remembered something. Do you want me to tell you what it was?" She slid her hand slowly up their thighs, so that all they could do was nod. "Well, I'm sure as firefighters you must have to study a *lot* about anatomy and such."

They nodded again.

She trailed her fingertips up onto their bellies. That stopped them. "Know what a G-spot is, boys?"

Again they both nodded.

"What *good* boys you are. Well, the G-spot is located at the front wall of a woman's *puuuuusssssy*." She drew the word out, trailing her fingers down the tops of their outside legs.

"Now last night, I was sleeping on my belly when my lover woke me and, *oooh,* that was how he fucked me, and, *oooooo,* that long. Hard. Cock." Her fingers circled back up the insides of their legs. Sweat dripped from Sean's nose and Andy's cleft chin. "It *stimmmm*-ulated my G-spot — remember, on the front of my body, and — " She gave a low moan. "It felt *soooo* good. It made me come *soooo* hard!"

Her fingers reached their crotches; she pushed underneath, cupping their balls, which jumped in her hands, evoking gasps as they spread their legs to give her easier access. *Such good boys.*

"And then," she sighed, feeling her own crotch beginning to overflow at the bounty before her, "I got fucked again. On my back this time."

One of them gasped.

"And it was slow. And sweet. And aaaaaagonizingly good, and he did it again, his cock making that little spot in my *pussy* feel... *Mmm....* I came again, so hard I passed out."

She looked up at them as she juggled their testicles. Their eyes were closed, their jaws slack. "Now, gentlemen, do you know what I've realized?"

They shook their heads.

"Oh, now, gentlemen, I think you have. I think you have figured out what it took me *allllllll* day to work out." She began to run her hands up the fronts of the pajamas. *Oh, yes. I got it. I win!* "Open your eyes please."

They both did, each gazing at her hand pressing against his crotch.

"Now, gentlemen, for this demonstration to work, you shouldn't be looking at your *own* equipment. Look at your roommate's."

Sean's gaze shifted smoothly to Andy's lap. Andy's locked pleadingly onto Lea's.

"Now, now, Andy, if you're a good boy, you know you'll get a reward, don't you?"

"Uh-huh," he gasped, sounding in fact very young. Very eager to please. And very horny. He pulled his eyes away from hers and looked down at where the tip of Sean's cock was pushing above the waistband of his pajama pants.

"Here's what I realized, gentlemen." Now she stroked their growing erections, urging them on. "I realized that I came twice from having my G-spot *stimulated.*" She slid each hand up to where each cock had now pushed out of the pajamas; she circled the tips with her fingers. "Once on my belly. And once on my back. And what does this tell us, gentlemen?"

"Both of us," sighed Sean, eyes half lidded but still locked on Andy's cock. "We both — *aah!*"

She had wrapped her hand around that long cock, which was now poking him in the belly button, and begun to stroke it.

He moaned and threw his head back, no longer able to watch.

As she continued to stroke him, she teased the uncircumcised head of Andy's, which was pushing away from his body as if desperate for more. "Do you see how good boys are rewarded, Andy?"

"Uh-huh." His eyes were still glued on the spectacle of Lea's hand milking Sean's long, freckled erection.

"Now," Lea pouted, "what I really want is one of these beautiful cocks in my *mouth*." She let loose a sigh. "But *then* I wouldn't be able to do as good a job with the other, and that wouldn't be any fun, would it?"

"Nuh-uh," they both grunted.

"I know! I'll suck the first one of you that helps me jerk the other off!"

Sean started to lift his hand, but — as Lea had guessed — Andy's shot out faster, grabbing Sean's erection at the base while she was at the head. Andy's hand slid up to meet Lea's, and then, together, they traveled down again. *Well, fuck, good thing you're so long, Sean!* she thought as they began to stroke him.

Sean screamed, and Lea felt a splash of pre-cum spill over her knuckles.

"What a *good* boy you are, Andy! If you help me just a *little more*... Look, Sean! Look at both our hands on your beautiful, long cock."

Seemingly against his will, Sean's eyes pushed themselves back open. "Aww... *Fuck*."

In unison, Lea and Andy sped up; Andy seemed to be as proficient and energetic at jacking off as he was at fucking, because Sean soon started thrusting into their hands. His cockhead was slick, and dark, dark red.

Suddenly, he stopped, held his breath, and..."*FUCK!*"

A rope of thick, white cum spewed over Lea's hand, landing in a long rivulet that started at one of Sean's nipples and ran down nearly to his navel.

Grinning up at him, Lea ran a finger through the cum and brought it to her lips. She licked it off. *"Mmm."*

"*Lea*," Andy whimpered.

"Don't worry, sweet boy. I'm going to give your reward now, don't you worry." Turning toward Andy, she worked to free his cock from the flannels that were holding it back; it was pushing out toward her like a dog pulling at its leash.

The PJs didn't want to let it go.

Finally, he pushed the offending pants down to his knees.

"Thanks, Andy," purred Lea, grasping his cock in both hands and bending forward to kiss the head.

"Damn," he gasped. "Good gawd *damn*."

Slowly, carefully — trying to think through how having a cock that curved down your throat was going to be different — she slowly sucked him in, and he continued to cuss a blue streak.

She discovered that actually, for such a big cock, Andy's was relatively easy to take into her mouth, because of the reverse curve.

She was just beginning to give herself over fully to giving him a blow job that would repay the mind-blowing fuck that he'd treated her to the night before when a hand began to slide up the inside of her thigh — from the back.

"Aw, sweetheart," whispered Sean into her ear. "You have no idea how fucking hot you look, that pretty mouth stretched around his big ol' thang."

She moaned, mouth full of *thang*, incredibly nimble fingers exploring her crotch.

"What reward'll you give *me*, Lea," Sean whispered on, his other hand gliding just over her belly, her breasts, "if I help you suck this country boy off."

Releasing the dick in question from her mouth but not her hands, she groaned, "Anything you fucking want."

"Anything?"

"Yup." Not wanting to lose herself in those blue eyes, in the feeling of those strong, gentle fingers on her flesh, or the thought of that cock… She went back to sucking on Andy's equally lovely pound of flesh.

"What I want, Lea," said Sean, fingers scintillating as he leaned forward with her and gave one of Andy's heavy balls a slow lick. "What I've wanted since I met you seven years ago…" He sucked the testicle into his mouth and released it, causing Andy to howl and a dollop of bitter pre-cum to splash into Lea's mouth. "What I want, baby, is *you*." He ran his tongue up the length of Andy's erection until his mouth met hers; together they devoured Andy, whose fingers tangled in both heads of hair.

And as they kissed around Andy's cock — a kiss that Lea too had been dreaming about for seven years, though she'd never anticipated the swelling cock head pressing between and through their lips — Sean moved Lea's panties smoothly to the side, slipped his once-more hard cock smoothly into her, and for a moment — just one endless, timeless moment — the whole fucking world was absolutely fucking *perfect*.

# The Visitor Comes Home

Lea was back in an airplane bathroom; her legs were down this time, and her panties were up; she was done using the facilities, and masturbation was the last thing on her mind — and the last thing that her body could handle.

Sean and Andy had made very sure that she'd had *all* that she could handle over the last three days. And nights.

Well, *more* than she could handle, which she wouldn't have thought possible. She wouldn't be walking straight for days. Probably wouldn't be able to touch herself for weeks. Well. Till the next day, anyway. Well. Okay. Until that night. If she were careful.

Not that she would be complaining any time soon.

But what she wasn't sure how to handle was how to explain any or all of this to her best friend and roommate, Kirsten — Sean's sister. Lea couldn't think of a good way to approach the fact that not only had Lea finally, *finally* bedded Kirsten's older brother, whom Lea'd crushed on and lusted after since the two women were still in college, but that they'd frolicked with *Sean's* roommate. Who, like Sean, was a tall, broad-shouldered, Southern firefighter. A wet dream on legs.

And that was quite outside the difficulty of letting Lea's best friend know that she would be leaving San Francisco at the end of the month, leaving Kirsten without a roommate.

It was overwhelming to feel so excited and *satisfied* at the same time as Lea felt nervous and *sore*.

The bell rang and the captain's voice rang out. "We've got some turbulence ahead. Please take your seats and buckle your seat belts. We'll try to keep this as smooth and as entertaining as possible."

*Thanks,* thought Lea. *Will you come home with me?*

•••

When Lea texted *Landed!* from the airport and didn't get a text back, she figured that Kirsten was at work; the Union Square store looked askance at pulling out your phone on the sales floor. Still, it would have been nice.

So Lea sent the same text to Sean and Andy and was gratified to receive *great miss u* from Andy and *WHEN ARE YOU COMING BACK????* from Sean. She was grinning from her head to her aching hamstrings as she boarded the BART train and texted back *Can't wait to come back there and burn down the REST of Dixie!*

Her two Georgia boys informed her that would never happen, not even if she brought Sherman and his whole army.

She informed them — as her bus approached her stop — that the only army she planned on encountering when she came back to Atlanta was the two of them, and she had every hope that the South would rise again. And again.

Which they solemnly promised her it would.

Backpack on her back, Lea was giggling — *giggling!* — as she made her way up to her floor, fished out her keys, and threw open the door to the crowded one-bedroom that she shared with Kirsten.

The apartment was small. Lea and Kirsten had learned to deal with this. They'd lived together before, were (mostly) compatible and (mostly) in sync, and so they'd learned how to avoid being walked in on — or being the one who walked in.

Obviously, the lesson hadn't stuck, because the sight that greeted Lea upon returning from her odyssey was her best friend, head thrown back in ecstasy, her blonde mane trailing along the length of the kitchen table, her legs wrapped over a pair of very fine, very feminine shoulders.

"*SORRY!*" shouted Lea before her brain could point out to her that she could simply have closed the door and come back later.

Kirsten's blue eyes — the same ridiculous, washed-denim blue as her brother's — flew open, as did Kirsten's mouth. The woman who was pleasuring Kirsten looked up into Kirsten's face, and then spun around on her knees and screamed, covering her body and bolting through the door to the apartment's miniscule bathroom, which she shut with a bang.

Kirsten and Lea stared at each other.

"I... I..." spluttered Kirsten.

"Sorry, I'll come back, oh, god, I'm so sorry!"

"No, Lea, wait," soft, long, Georgia vowels called out.

Head whirling, Lea turned to the front door, took a breath and closed it. "You, um, want to put some clothes on?"

Behind Lea, Kirsten chuckled. "Kinda late for that."

Lea turned and tried to return her friend's grin. Given how awkward Kirsten's smile looked and how brightly Kirsten was blushing from head to mid-thigh, Lea figured she was doing a pretty good job of approximating it.

"Um," Kirsten began, then shook her head and chuckled. "Thought you were coming back tomorrow."

"Nope."

"Guess not."

The friends both laughed, and Lea felt her heart begin to descend from her throat when she made out a quiet, sustained sniffle from the bathroom.

Kirsten grimaced and went over to the bathroom door. "Hey, Gianna, sweety? You want your clothes?"

"Please." The voice from behind the door was very small and very moist.

Lea picked up the skirt, top, and undies at her feet that looked nothing like anything she'd ever seen Kirsten wear and raised an eyebrow at her friend.

Kirsten shrugged and took the clothes, turning to the bathroom door and knocking. "Here y'are, sweetie." She passed the clothes through.

Lea found herself staring at her friend's naked back, at the freckles that were so much like the ones she'd been staring at — licking — just that morning. She shook her head, trying to clear it.

The bathroom door opened. Gianna turned out to be a very petite woman. She shuffled out, her eyes downcast.

Kirsten turned to Lea, tits high, as if they were meeting at a formal ball. "Gianna, I've told you about my friend Lea. Lea…" Kirsten's eyes widened slightly. "This is my… my girlfriend Gianna."

Lea and Gianna both glanced at Kirsten before looking at each other.

"Nice to meet you," said Lea.

"Pleasure," said Gianna, almost managing a smile before her dark skin darkened several shades. "Call me, K. Bye," she murmured to Kirsten, kissing the blonde on the lips very briefly before disappearing out the door.

Lea finally dropped her backpack to the floor.

"Welcome home?" Kirsten flashed a dazzling, off-center smile.

"Thanks. Kirsten? Girlfriend?"

"Uh, yeah." The blush that had begun finally to recede on Kirsten's fair skin came roaring back.

"I mean," Lea said, "that's great, but... Wow. Since when?"

"'Bout a month." When she noticed Lea's shocked expression, Kirsten shrugged. "Well, honey, you've been a bit pre-occupied with the whole job search. And... Anyway. Yeah."

"So, girls?"

"Yup."

"Did you just —?"

"Oh, gawd, no. She's not the first or anything."

"*Really?*"

Blushing fully now, Kirsten turned and walked into their kitchen. "Um, naw. Remember Billy?"

"The guy with the thing for handcuffs?"

"Yeah, but, see, um, more of a Billie-with-an-i-e than a Billy-with-a-y." Kirsten grabbed a bottle of Pinot Gris out of the fridge and poured two large water glasses full.

"Oh." Fuck. That had been... Just after college! No wonder Kirsten had never brought him — her — over. "Why didn't you ever *say* anything?"

Kirsten's shoulder's slumped. "Some of us don't come from liberal San Fran families, sweetie." She handed Lea one glass of wine and sipped at the other.

"Kirsten..."

"Yeah, well, see, also, see, I mean I've always liked guys too, but see, I've known I've liked girls a long time, only I didn't actually think that was anything I could, you know, do something about until college."

"So? You could have told me!"

Kirsten favored Lea with a miserable smirk. "Sweetie. You're my best friend. And that's why I couldn't."

Lea just stared at Kirsten.

"Gawd, Lea, don't..." Kirsten looked away, took a drink, and put down the glass. "I couldn't tell you, sweetie, 'cause, you know, besides being my roommate and my BFF and all that shit, you have a cute fucking ass and I had a huge fucking crush on you that confused the shit out of me, okay?"

"Uh. Okay?" Lea tried to consider whether any of this upset her or weirded her out. Nope. Well, it did make Kirsten's whole obsession with helping Lea choose her underwear seem a bit less benign. But other than that... nope.

"And I still love you, but no, not like *that*. I mean, I figured out real quick you were just about the straightest girl on God's green earth, so I haven't been lusting after you all these years, which I didn't want you to have to think about, which is another reason why I didn't tell you, okay?"

Lea clicked her glass to her friend's. "Okay, K. I got it. I'm sorry."

Kirsten laughed. "*Sorry?* What the hell for?"

"That you didn't feel like you could just tell me."

"Aw, honey, I probably should have long ago. I mean, I guess I knew you wouldn't mind, I just..." She shrugged again.

"Hey, no prob." Lea frowned. "I'd give you a hug, but that seems like it would be sending the wrong signal."

Kirsten gave a sad smirk and shook her head. "Yeah. How 'bout I get some clothes on?"

"If you think it would help." A laugh fought its way up Lea's throat. "Thought you said it was too late?"

"Yeah, well, your damn city is cold, and anyway, I'm feeling kinda stupid standing here butt-naked." She walked around the table and picked up her dress.

"So. Gianna? Seems... nice."

For the first time that Lea could remember, Kirsten turned away as she got dressed. "She is, a real sweetie."

"Hope I didn't scare her off."

"Me too. Actually, that's another thing I probably shoulda talked to you about before now." Kirsten turned around, fully dressed but uncharacteristically timid.

Lea walked over and gave her a hug — fuck sending the wrong message. "Talked to me about what?"

"Well, see..." After a moment's hesitation, Kirsten hugged her back. "See, we've gotten kinda serious, the last few weeks, and, see, she's got this nice little place on Leavenworth, just a few blocks from the store, and, um..."

Lea backed up and looked at her friend, whose expression had gone from humiliated to thoroughly miserable. "What? You... You want to move in with her?"

"Um. Yeah?" Kirsten's brows bowed down. "But see, I didn't want to leave you having to pay for this place on your own, so — "

Lea laughed and hugged her friend, so that some of the wine poured down Lea's back. "And here I was worried about having to tell *you!*"

"Tell...?" Then Kirsten gasped. "Oh! Sweetie! You got the job?"

"Yup!"

"That's so great! Hey! Congratulations!" Now Kirsten gave Lea a real hug. "Wow! Can't wait to tell Sean!"

"Um. He already knows."

Kirsten pulled back from her friend and peered into her face. "Oh?" Kristen began to grin.

Now it was Lea's turn to blush.

Kirsten gave a whoop and hugged Lea again. "Are you telling me you and Big Bro finally got off y'all's asses and got *lucky?*"

"Oh, boy, yeah." Lea knew that she was turning bright red, but she too was laughing; it was hard not to laugh with Kirsten — or with her brother, for that matter.

"Thank *gawd!*" Kirsten gave Lea another squeeze and went to refill her wine, most of which she'd now spilled. "If I had to listen to the two of y'all *lust* after each other any more — " Kirsten turned back and shot Lea a supremely wicked grin. "So? Was it good? Did y'all fuck each other's brains out? I mean, I don't want details, this is my brother and all, but *still.* Dish, girl!"

"Um. Yeah. God. Kirsten!" That morning, in the back of Andy's Yukon, Sean licking Lea's pussy while Andy suckled on her nipples… They had made her feel exactly as if she had just had not one but two amazing men pleasure her in every way imaginable for three whole days and nights. Which in fact she had. Lea could barely bend her own brain about what had happened. She couldn't even begin to think how to tell her best friend, who happened to be one of her lovers' sister. She figured that nothing that she could say would come anywhere near to the truth.

"Wow," laughed Kirsten. "I always thought Big Bro was the mushy, romantic type. Didn't figure he'd fuck you speechless!"

"Had help," Lea muttered.

She hadn't meant to say it out loud, and so she was shocked when her friend blinked at her. "Say *what?*"

"Uh." Lea hid behind her glass of wine.

"No, no, no, Miss Lea, you don't get to drop a little bomb like that and then play *peek-a-boo!*" Kirsten squinted through Lea's Pinot Gris. "Now, did you say what I *thought* you said?"

Lea sighed. She'd figured that — if the arrangement continued, as it showed every sign of doing — she was going to have to tell Kirsten eventually. She just hadn't planned on blurting it out quite so soon. "What did you think I said?"

Kirsten made a face that was even more contorted viewed through the glass. "Sounded like maybe you and Sean had some *company.*"

Lea just nodded.

"Well, damn! What did…?" Kirsten gasped, reached out, and moved Lea's glass to the side. "Please tell me it was Andrew."

Again, all that Lea could do was nod.

"Holy fuck." Beyond that statement, Kirsten was speechless — a rare occurrence. After a moment she recovered. "I mean, those big country boys don't usually do a *thang* for me, but he is a beautiful piece of man-flesh, sure enough."

"Tell me about it," sighed Lea.

"No, honey, *you* tell *me!*" Kirsten laughed, then shook her head and held up her hand. "I mean, naw, bleh, don't. Don't wanna hear about it if Sean was... I mean, are we talking, you know, *both* of them?"

"Uh-huh."

"At the *same time?*"

"Well," Lea said, fidgeting, "first night it was one, then the other." She shivered, remembering the two mind-scrambling fucks, remembering the thunder. "But after I got the job..."

"Holy fuck," Kirsten said again, looking properly stunned. She bit her lip. "Um. Did Sean and Andrew...?" She pointed her index fingers at each other, sloshing some more wine.

"I think I'm going to let *Sean* tell you about that." Lea took a deep breath and a sip of wine. "And you can tell him about Gianna."

"Wow. Uh. Yeah." Kirsten drank from her glass, and shook her head again. "There's a conversation our mama won't ever want to hear about. And here I always thought Sean was the good one in the family."

"Oh," laughed Lea, "I think you're both wonderful."

• • •

As it turned out Lea *hadn't* scared Gianna off. Though the petite brunette seemed very calm when she picked Kirsten up to go to dinner, however, Gianna still couldn't look Lea in the face.

"You sure you don't want to join us, Lea?" Kirsten asked for the third time.

"No, I think I've interrupted you two enough for today," answered Lea, and after a moment all three women laughed. Even Gianna.

After they had left, Lea sighed and shuffled her way over to the fridge. Three heads of lettuce — the red leaf badly wilted, but the romaine and the butter lettuce still looking good — her choice of eight kinds of hummus, and a few leftover falafel. No pita, but some whole-grain tortilla — instant dinner.

As she pulled her plate together and moved over to the table — aware only after she already eaten most of her meal that she'd sat at the spot where Gianna had been dining on Kirsten earlier that day — she sighed, knowing she was going to miss California's food. *But Atlanta's a big city,* she reasoned, *I'm sure I can get good food.* Then she giggled as she thought, *And I sure know I can find some great meat there!*

After eating Lea retired to the bedroom she had shared with Kirsten since breaking up with John the Control Freak a bit over a year before. She started to watch *30 Rock*, but found that she kept glancing over at her roomie's bed. Would it be any different sharing a room with Kirsten now that Lea knew that her friend liked girls — had had a crush on Lea herself? Well, that had been years before. Kirsten was obviously fine with it. And they'd made (and so far kept) an agreement when they'd roomed together in college: no bringing anyone else into the bedroom without giving the other a chance to clear out.

Lea had just started to wonder whether she should look for another place to spend the night so Kirsten and Gianna could have some privacy, when Lea's phone chirped. A text from Kirsten read, *Spending the night at G's. OK?*

Smiling, Lea texted back, *Great. Have a nice sleepover. ;-)*

*LOL! ILU!* came back the response almost instantly.

As she was putting her phone back down, ready to dive back into the ever-entertaining travails of Liz Lemon, Lea's phone chirped again.

It was from Sean this time: *Hey, miss you. Both of us do.*

Lea's chest filled with warmth. She answered, *I miss you both too. Wanna see us?*

*?*

*Video chat. On the computer. Andy wants to be able to see too, for some reason.*

Lea laughed, imagining the two burly boys fighting over the little phone. She flipped open her laptop. *Okay. Tell me when.*

*Now?* And he gave a link.

Lea entered it into her browser. The feed loaded... "Holy shit."

Two broad-chested, naked male bodies greeted her, visible from the neck down, so she wasn't immediately sure which was which. They were sitting on the edge of the pullout, knees spread, each stroking the other's cock.

Yes. The one on the right had a cock that curved away from his body: Andy.

"Holy fuck," she repeated.

"Nice to see you too," one of them murmured – over the tiny laptop speakers, she thought it was Sean, but wasn't certain.

"Guess you guys couldn't wait."

"Told you we missed you," said the other one, accent a bit heavier, so that had to be Andy.

"Uh-huh." Lea could feel warmth spread through her middle, could feel her still-sore pussy moistening and her nipples reaching out through her blouse toward the screen. "So... Tell me, boys, what part of me did you miss?" And before they could answer, she began to unbutton her top.

Stripping had always seemed like a silly exercise to Lea. She was a practical girl: the whole taking-clothes-off thing just got in the way on the way from foreplay to *play*. But men, she knew, were visual souls — and her boys, clearly, were men. As Lea slowly opened the front of her sensible blouse, their stroking slowed, and they visibly leaned forward.

Besides, this was the best they could give each other until next month.

Once the last button was undone, she slid a finger all of the way back up her torso. "Did you miss my neck?"

"Yes, ma'am," said one. "Uh-huh," said the other.

Taking the collar, Lea pulled the blouse away from one side. "My shoulders?"

This time, they both just grunted their assent.

Lea pouted down at her own flesh. "Someone clearly misses it — they left teeth marks there."

There was a hiss from the speakers.

Lea slid the other shoulder free. "No marks there though. Guess you don't miss this one as much."

"Nuh-uh," groaned one of the boys.

"Miss that one too," said the other. "Lots."

"Mmm." Lea slid the bra strap on that side down. "You sure?"

"Yes," they groaned together. Their hands had begun moving minutely more quickly.

"You sure you miss my left as much as you miss my right?" Down slipped the other bra strap.

"Oh, fuck yes," said one.

"Huh" was all the other could manage.

Lea let the blouse slide off of her, down to the bed. "What else have you missed?"

"Uh..."

She held the bra up with one hand and trailed the other downward. "My belly? I see some marks there too — you must miss that."

"Damn."

"Yeah."

Grinning, she turned away from the screen. "Tell me, did you leave any marks on my back?"

And before they could even grunt, she added, "Oh! But you can't see the whole back. Here." She popped her bra open and let it join the top on her comforter. "Miss my back?"

"You know we did."

"Love... bites."

Lea wriggled, pretending to try to look over her shoulder. "Ooo, really? I wonder whose?"

"Pro'lly both," one of them grunted.

"I sure hope so," she said. "But have you checked my *whole* back?"

"Uh...."

She got up on her knees. "How about... down here?" She pushed her jeans down an inch.

"Um."

"Don't... see nothing."

"Oh, what a shame." She popped the button on the jeans and slid them another inch down. "How about... here?"

"Um, maybe."

"Can't quite, um, see."

"Well, we wouldn't want to have that." She bent forward, wriggling the jeans and panties down so that her whole ass was pointing at the screen.

"Sweet Jesus."

"Fuck."

Lea couldn't help it. She laughed. "Guess you do miss this part. Don't think either of you took full... possession, though."

Groans answered her, and the sound of each pounding the other's cock.

Stepping out of the jeans, she bent all of the way forward. "This part, though?" She reached between her legs and gently stroked herself. "This part? Oh, guys, you sure as hell took possession of this part of me."

Whimpering.

"This part of me? It misses you both too. Sooooo much..." Gingerly, she slid a finger in, and was amazed that it felt so good. "You guys fucked my lights out, but my poor little pussy is still weeping for more." Another finger. Lea hissed; it stung a bit, but honestly, it was true. She wanted it. God help her: she wanted *them*. She peered back between her legs and saw them stroking each other on her little laptop screen — another wet dream come to life.

Andy was rocking his hips, thrusting into Sean's hand. Lea could tell that he was close.

Apparently, so could Sean. Disengaging Andy's hand from his own erection, Sean knelt to the floor, staring first at Lea — Lea's bottom, spread for both of them to see, Lea's fingers thrusting slowly in and out — and then staring up at Andy. Sean kissed Andy's slick cockhead. "You can think about think about fucking that sweet poon there," he rumbled, "an' come in my mouth. If you'll let me come in yours." He gave Andy's cock a lick, from balls to head.

Andy gasped. Though he'd seemed to be okay touching Sean's rod, he'd been much less comfortable letting any part of his body other than his hand touch Sean anywhere — certainly not his mouth, and certainly not Sean's cock.

Lea wanted to be patient and kind, wanted not to force Andy to do something he clearly wasn't totally comfortable doing. But the sight of Sean on his knees between their lover's legs, licking his way up their lover's cock — it left Lea with no patience. No kindness. "Oh, Andy," she moaned, sliding her fingers in and out, arching her ass, "want you in me *so bad*…"

Sean's mouth reached the top of that long prick, and stayed there.

*"GAWD,"* cried Andy, all restraint breaking, as he began to thrust into his friend's mouth. "Gawd, fuck, *fine*, *SHIT*, you can stick that *thang* in my mouth, *FUCK*, just, just let…"

Sean showed that he had been paying close attention when he'd been helping her suck Andy off. Smoothly, Sean took an astonishing amount of that long *thang* of Andy's down his throat.

"God," moaned Lea, "so fucking beautiful." Her thumb was trembling as it stroked her clit. "Fuck me, Andy."

And fuck her he did — fucking Sean's face as he grimaced at her, her cunt, at the fingers stretching it….

"Oh, fuck, fuck, fuck me, Andy, fuck me…!"

Andy screamed and arched, thrusting hard. Once. Twice. Then he collapsed back onto the bed. "Aw, fuck. Fuck."

Sean came coughing up, wiping his face. "Well, damn, boy, you just about broke my spine from the inside!"

"Aw, fuck…" Andy was still lying back, his cock leaning drunkenly down over his thigh.

Sean slid up next to Andy, and for a terrible, scintillating moment Lea was sure that Sean, the mushy romantic as Kirsten had said, was about to kiss his roommate. But after a second, Sean just reached down and gave Andy's softening cock a squeeze. "Andy-boy, you don't have to — "

Andy's hand shot out and grabbed Sean's, which was still hard. Sean gulped, and Lea gasped in sympathy.

"Y'all both sucked me off how many time?" rasped Andy, stroking his friend's prick. "I mean, if you can take *me* in y'all's mouths, shouldn't be no big deal to take *this* little ol' thang in mine, right?"

"*Little?*" Sean scowled, and (upside down as she was) Lea couldn't tell if he were kidding or not.

But Andy didn't volley back. Instead he rolled on his stomach and held Sean's cock steady before him. He stared at it as if it were a stick of dynamite, liable to go off at any second. He leaned forward, face stony, and gave the head a kiss.

Sean pushed up on his elbows; his eyes darted between Andy, who had backed up and was now licking his lips, and over Andy's back at Lea, who was trying to assuage the fire in her loins as gingerly as she could.

Andy opened his mouth wide, as if he were about to begin a hot-dog eating competition — which, in a way, he was — but Lea had enough brain left to whimper, "Teeth."

Andy blinked up at Lea, and then back down. "Oh. Right." He carefully covered his teeth with his lips, closed his eyes, and took the tip of Sean's cock in his mouth.

It wasn't an expert blowjob, but Lea could remember her own first attempt, and gave Andy an A for diving right in.

Sean looked stunned. He still couldn't seem to figure out where to look: at Lea's open cunt on the computer screen, or at his friend's open mouth, bobbing up and down on his cock.

Lea decided that he deserved a bit of torture as well. "Feel good, Sean?"

His eyes flashed up to the webcam and locked on hers.

Lea flexed her ass, grinding on her own hand. "Looks so fucking hot, Andy sucking you off. Don't you think so, Sean?"

Sean growled. Scowled. But his eyes flashed down.

Lea grinned, astonished to feel an orgasm beginning to build up in her tired pussy. "Wish I was there... *Mmm...* Wish I was there to help Andy... Or... Or I could... *Mmmm*... Could suck on him while he.... *Hnh....! While* he, um, sucked on you, and.... Is he, uh, *god*, is Andy getting hard again, Sean?"

Eyes smoldering, Sean slipped his hand under Andy, grabbing something that made Andy lift his pelvis up, revealing that, yes, he was hard again, and yes, what Sean had grabbed hold of and was once more stroking was that gorgeous cock of Andy's.

"Oh, *fuck,* Sean, god... And you could use that amazing mouth of yours on *this*..." She arched her pelvis again, opening herself to him, thrilled and terrified to find herself sliding another finger in; she could feel the muscles protest, could feel them exult. "God, Sean, Andy, want you so much, *want....!*" She began to buck against one hand as she sucked the other into her mouth, seeking *fullness,* seeking completion such as only those two had ever given her...

Sean screamed. Her name, maybe. Or maybe the Supreme Being's. Or hell, maybe Andy's.

Lea couldn't tell, because to her own great and wonderful shock, she came, hard, squeezing tight the three fingers in her snatch, screaming into the fingers in her mouth.

Once she had returned to her body, Lea curled her knees to her belly and rolled onto her side, staring at the screen.

Her two boys were there, slick with sweat. Andy had come still dribbling down his chin, but he was hard in Sean's hand. Each was slack-jawed. Each was staring back at her.

Lea felt tears overflow — something she'd promised herself she wouldn't let happen. "Miss you both so much."

"Love you," they both murmured to her together, and Lea surrendered herself to the tears.

That night, they could barely say anything else to each other than to agree to talk again the next night. "Can't do it like this," mumbled Andy.

Sean added, "We're at the firehouse the next three nights."

"Oh," sighed Lea — sorry, even as her body was relieved.

The next night, they chatted briefly, both men looking very businesslike in their Atlanta FD t-shirts. The laptop was on Andy's knees, and so it felt as if Lea were looking up at them. It made her feel oddly small. It made her feel... oddly safe.

"Anyone else there with you guys?" Lea asked.

Andy's eyes flashed up, over the top of the computer, while Sean simply nodded.

"Oh, shoot," Lea pouted.

They both grinned sadly at her.

"Hey," said Sean, "Sis and I had... a really interesting conversation earlier tonight."

Kirsten was once again over at Gianna's. Lea grinned, relieved that the siblings had in fact not made her bring it up. "Did she tell you who *she's* moving in with?"

Sean scratched his head. "Uh. Yeah."

Andy looked at him quizzically.

Lea laughed. "Put it to you this way, Andy, their mama is going to have lot easier time swallowing her boy sharing a girl with you than her *girl* being with a — "

" — with a, yeah," Sean broke in, and whispered into Andy's ear.

Andy's eyes got very wide.

Lea laughed. "Yup! Kirsten told me that conversation was one your mother would probably be better off never hearing about."

"Well, she had that just about right."

"Hey." Lea felt her mischievous side rising. "I know there's other guys there, but they can't see the screen, can they?"

Both boys shook their heads.

"Good," said Lea, and lifted her shirt over her head.

Their twin stunned expressions was all the payment she wished for... that night.

Two nights before it was time for Lea to fly back to them, Lea got on their now-nightly chat full of excitement. She'd shipped boxes of belongings to their place — her place soon — had put in her last day at the tiny theater she'd managed to keep from folding, and had helped Kirsten finish moving into Gianna's. She had the bare apartment to herself, had nothing to do tomorrow but pack and see a few friends, and tonight her boys were home — the next night they were on duty.

She looked forward to a long, leisurely video threeway, their last, thank god, for a long time, because, really, she was ready to have them both take her again. And again.

She anticipated them being naked, as they had been every other night when they were at their apartment. Had anticipated watching them sucking each other off. Maybe, a secret, very adolescent part of her hoped, she could encourage one of them to let the other fuck him if she offered her own ass as a reward. The thought of taking one of those very sizable cocks up her backside was more than a little terrifying, but....

When she got online at the appointed time, however, both boys were sitting, still fully clothed in their fire department duds. Both very serious. Each holding a piece of paper.

"Guys?" Lea asked, nervous at their unaccounted solemnity. "Everything okay?"

They nodded, still grim-faced. Andy held up his piece of paper. "Got the results of our physicals back."

"Oh?" *What the hell?*

"Look in your inbox," said Sean, and that serious face suddenly had a spark of something smoldering beneath it.

Nervous, Lea opened her email. There was a message from Sean with two PDFs attached. She double-clicked on them.

At the bottom of each was the blood screening.

Sean was O+. Andy was A+. Both had good cholesterol; Andy's HDL was marginally higher. Neither tested positive for any of several cancer markers.

Each had tested negative for HIV, HPV, genital herpes, syphilis, gonorrhea, and any one of a number of other communicable diseases.

They were clean.

Not certain why they were sharing this with her, she looked up at them. "Guys?"

They were both staring back at her. Andy's gaze too was full of banked flame now. "Wanted you to know," he said, "that you didn't need to worry."

"We'll still wear rubbers and all when we're, you know," Sean's face darkened, "fucking. But…"

"You don't need to worry," repeated Andy.

A thick gobbet of emotion stopped Lea's throat for a moment. "What about… you guys… worrying about *me*?"

"We trust you," said Andy.

"Also," added Sean, that wicked smile of his creeping in, "I know from Sis that you hadn't had, uh, intimate contact before us with anyone over the last two years except for John the Controlling Asshole. And he always wore rubbers 'cause — "

" — because he didn't want any Little Johns running around without his permission," finished Lea, trying but failing to match his smile. "Uh, guys?"

"Darlin'?"

"Baby?"

"I renewed my prescription for, um, The Pill."

Sean's eyebrows raised. "So…"

Andy licked his lips. "So…"

Love and desire swept through Lea. "So. Gentlemen. Next time I see you in the flesh, I am *soo* going to be able to feel both of you go off inside me. At the same time."

"Well…" Sean murmured.

"Golly," gulped Andy.

And each began to pull his t-shirt over his head as Lea unzipped the hoodie that was all that she was wearing tonight.

*I'm going home!* she sighed to herself, and then groaned as her two gorgeous, sweet men each pulled the other's pants off and began to stroke the other hard.

# The Visitor Comes Again

Lea had just lowered her skirt and stood up when the captain came on the intercom and said, "Ladies and gentlemen, they've cleared the runway, and so we are now descending into Hartsfield-Jackson Atlanta International Airport. Please take your seats."

Out in the cabin, there was cheering — there had been threats of diverting to Miami.

In the bathroom, Lea was having a panic attack.

Fuckity-fuck-fuck. What was she *doing*?

Well, she thought, as she made her way back to her seat, she was moving to Atlanta for her new job, which started in just a week's time. The job she'd been dreaming of, at a theater she was overjoyed to be working at. She was going to have a *staff,* for fuck's sake! She wasn't going to *be* the whole staff — and the janitor, and the concessions-stand dishwasher, and...

And she was moving into her new apartment. Moving in with Sean. And Andy. Sean and Andy.

Thinking of Sean and Andy — her two boys, her two *men* — who, damn it, wouldn't be able to see her until tomorrow because they were, damn it, *working* — got her middle moving again, but this time it wasn't anxiety. She was thinking of the feeling of two cocks in her hands. Of one of them in her cunt while the other filled her mouth. Of Sean helping her suck Andy dry. Of the two of them whispering, "Love you," over the video chats that had been her life-line to them over the past few weeks.

Of the fact that she was *moving in* with two men whom she'd only really gotten to know over three days of bacchanalian orgy — well, and two weeks of passionate (if wistful) video-fucking.

She'd lived with men before. Roommates. Boyfriends.

But two of them *at once?* One she'd known for years, but how well? He was her best friend's brother, but really? What did she know about Sean?

And *Andy?* What did she know about him at all?

Well. That he came from Smoky Mountains. That he liked boiled peanuts. That he made really good fried chicken.

That his cock bent away from his body, and he could make her come *so* hard....

It wasn't a whole hell of a lot.

She had her key in her purse. They'd made up the big sofa-sleeper for her use — and theirs, once they were off duty.

They were good guys. Good boys.

But she was going to have to make her way through — of all things — a snow-bound Atlanta, and then she was going to spend her first night in the apartment alone. Which shouldn't feel shitty — Lea liked being alone — but it did. Feel shitty.

The downside of living with two firefighters was definitely going to be that they had twenty-four hour shifts.

The upside, she knew, was that they only had two of them a week. Which left them the rest of the week to make Lea feel like a very, very natural woman indeed, thank you, Carole King.

*Still*, thought Lea with an internal pout, *couldn't they have managed to have today off?*

"Your boyfriend meeting you in Atlanta?" asked the grey-haired black woman in the floral print dress sitting in the window seat.

Not feeling like it was worth the trouble of explaining the complicated mess she was walking into, Lea just nodded.

"Thought so," tittered the woman. "I've seen *that* look before!" She graced Lea with a a self-satisfied smile. And before Lea could say anything, she turned back to her copy of *Fifty Shades*.

Fuckity-fuck-fuck.


As they descended into Atlanta, Lea found that *fifty shades of grey* was about right: the city, which had been verdant the last time she'd flown in just a few weeks before, was now monochromatic. Flat.

The lady next to Lea seemed to be just as disconcerted. "Why, will you look at that? If it's global *warming* what the hell is Atlanta doing looking like *that?*"

Lea decided not to get into a debate about climate change — it didn't seem like anything good would come from that. "Do you have someone picking you up?" she asked.

"Oh, yes, bless you, my oldest boy will be there. He's got a big ol' four-by-four pickup." She patted Lea on the knee with a mahogany hand. "He's a fireman."

Lea fought back a wave of irrational panic. She *knew* this lady wasn't one of the ladies she'd one day have to explain just how she'd contributed to her beautiful, upstanding son's downfall. She'd met Sean's mother, who was as fair and freckled as her children, and Andy was if anything paler. It seemed unlikely that he would have an African American mom. Still… "I… I'm seeing a fireman." *I am,* thought Lea with a guilty, swallowed giggle, *TWO of them!* "Midtown."

"Oh, how nice! My boy's down in East Point." The woman's hand flapped against Lea's knee again. "I'm sure they know each other!"

Lea tried to keep the nascent panic out of her smile. "I'm sure they do." *Oh, God,* Lea thought once more, *what am I doing?*

The plane touched down smoothly, though Lea's stomach still lurched — more from the fact that she was already close to throwing up than anything. The other passengers cheered.

Lea sat back and closed her eyes.

"Well, honey," burbled Lea's seatmate, "here we are!"

"Here we are," Lea agreed, voice thin even to her own ears.

As they shuffled up the big metal tube to the terminal, Lea could see her breath. *Weird,* she thought, and *How the fuck I'm I going to get to the apartment?* She had a rental car waiting for her, but there was sure to be ice, the car was almost certainly not going to have chains, and Lea wasn't exactly used to driving in winter conditions.

For the four hundred and thirty-second time, Lea found herself wishing that even one of her boys had been able to pick her up. They both drove four-wheel drive cars, but beside that, Lea just wanted to *see* them. She felt pathetic.

"Well, now," said Lea's former neighbor, "you'll have someone to warm you right up soon enough." The woman laughed. "You give that fireman of yours a big squeeze for me, you hear?"

Lea nodded, trying to smile. She found herself trembling, and the cold had almost nothing to do with it.

As they entered the terminal, the woman patted Lea on the shoulder and strode off through the sea of disgruntled passengers, her copy of *50 Shades of Grey* held proudly to her chest.

Lea stepped out of the flow of traffic and closed her eyes, leaning against one of the glass walls that looked out at the plane she had just left. *It will be all right. I'll get to the apartment okay. I'll survive one more night with no one to keep me warm. And then tomorrow...*

"Excuse me, miss," said a low, gruff voice. A heavy hand touched Lea's forearm, which was clutching her purse to her chest. "Would you mind coming with us?"

Lea's eyes flew open. The hand on her arm was gloved — heavy, industrial gloves — and attached to an arm clad in a heavy, buff-colored coat marked *Atlanta Fire & Rescue*. Blinking, she followed the arm...

It was attached to Andy. Andy, in his full turnout gear — coat, overalls, helmet.

And behind him, Sean.

Both of them somber-faced, but each with a joyously evil glint in his eye.

Lea started to squeal, to leap at them both, to see if she could rap her arms and legs around both of them at once — to hell with people watching — but Andy's hand held her fast. "I... I thought you were working!"

"We are," answered Sean. His posture said *On duty*, but his eyes promised pleasure, a promise that Lea's body immediately began urging her to collect on. "Obviously."

"We managed to *volunteer* for an extra shift out here at the airport," Andy added quietly, and then said more loudly. "We just need you to identify something for us, miss, if you'd just follow us."

"Identify?"

"Yes, miss." Andy winked, and gestured down the terminal — not in the direction of baggage claim, but toward one of the thousands of doors that you never notice as you wander through an airport.

Andy led and Lea followed; she could hear Sean taking up the rear — an image that set *all* sorts of nasty thoughts going in Lea's nasty, nasty mind. Andy used a key to open the door and waved the other two through into a small stairwell.

As soon as the door *clicked* shut, Lea turned and leapt, grabbing both men's collars, wrapped her legs around both of them — as best she could, since even without these heavy coats on they were not exactly small guys — and proceeded to kiss them both soundly. Two big hands reached under her butt, each holding up one cheek, each pulling her tight.

After a few minutes — not long enough, *never* long enough — Andy backed away from her neck and Sean backed away from her ear. "Guess you did miss us," chuckled Sean.

She glared at him and then grinned. "What do *you* think?"

"I think," Sean murmured, "that we missed the fuck out of you too, begging your pardon."

Her grin grew. She pushed her hand down between the two men, feeling their erections pressing together through the heavy overalls. "So, gentlemen. You had something you wanted me to *identify*."

Sean hissed.

Andy grunted through gritted teeth, "Not here. Security cameras all over."

"Oh?" Lea pushed her hand down again and wriggled against them. "You don't think the TSA would want to watch me take both of you in my mouth at the same — ?"

Sean stopped that mouth with a hair-curling kiss. He turned and pressed her up against the cold concrete wall, and Lea was just as happy that it was cold, because she wasn't sure that that Sean's heat wouldn't have vaporized her.

She heard a loud *thwack!* Sean broke the kiss and snarled at Andy, "Hey! Keep your hands to yourself!"

Andy smirked at them both, panting steam into the stairwell. "Come on, you two. Let's take this somewhere a bit more private."

• • •

*Somewhere a bit more private* turned out to be a ready room for the AFRD's airport battalion. "There's one in each terminal," Sean said as they made their way through an endless maze of corridors. "This one happens to be assigned just for us for today."

"How... convenient." Lea was walking between the two men, her arms hooked through their arms. She'd never been more conscious of just how much bigger than she they were. "A nice coincidence that you happened to be housed in the terminal where my flight landed."

"Isn't it?" Andy chuckled. "We may owe a few favors."

"Oh." Lea looked from one to the other. "Well, I hope that it was worth the trouble. I mean, doing all of that *just* so that you could see me when I got in…" She was teasing them, but in all honesty she truly was deeply touched.

"It was our pleasure," said Sean.

"We couldn't wait to see you," said Andy.

Two maintenance workers sauntered past in the opposite direction.

"Well, then," Lea sighed, "I suppose I'll just have to do my best to make sure that it was all worth your while."

"Er," said Andy.

"Huh," said Sean.

Lea just smiled and pulled their arms closer.

After what seemed like hours of meandering aimlessly through a labyrinth of anonymous corridors, they stopped at a door that looked exactly like several hundred other doors that they'd passed, except that this one bore a placard reading *AFRD BATT 7.*

As Andy pulled out the key, Lea asked, "BATT 7?"

"Battalion 7. That's the airport battalion," Sean answered.

"Wow. A whole other battalion. You guys *do* owe some favors." Lea grinned at him in a way that she hoped promised *just* how much she was going to make it worth their while.

*Such good boys!*

Sean grinned back, and it was his most wicked, pulse-quickening grin. "You have no idea."

A not-very-nice thought occurred to Lea. "You didn't promise anyone… *me*, did you?"

Sean's face fell, and Andy, who had just opened the door, turned around looking if anything even more abashed. "Lea! We wouldn't!"

She shivered, suddenly feeling the cold of the concrete floor flood up through her.

Sean led her through the open door; Andy closed it behind him with a *thud*.

Lea found suddenly that she couldn't look them in the face. She was staring at the battered, red industrial carpet.

Sean knelt so that he was looking up into her eyes. "Lea. It isn't like that. Honest."

"You think we'd *share* you?" Andy knelt beside Sean. "Like we'd share a truck or a hound?"

"You're pretty comfortable sharing me with each other," Lea joked — though it was a pathetic attempt even to her own ears.

"It ain't like that at all," said Andy, looking deadly serious. "It's not *sharing*, it's… I mean…" He reached a hand to her hip.

Sean took her other hip and, in fact, it felt as if they had rooted her back to the ground. "This is how we *get* to be with you, Lea-honey. And all," he added quietly, blinking at Andy, who blinked back.

"Lucky me." She was smiling, but she could feel that she was on the edge of tears. *Why?* "Sorry." She reached out and ran fingers through two heads of fine, blond hair. She was glad that they'd hung up their helmets — she could see them hanging on hooks by the door. Her boys in their gear, looking incredibly sexy… It was wonderful, but she was glad to be able to see their faces.

"What've you got to be sorry about?" Andy's hand drifted up to her ribs, sending predictable but unpredicted sparks to her nipples.

Sean leaned forward and kissed the point of Lea's hipbone, and that sent sparks further south.

Astonished to find the cold vacuum that had threatened to consume her filling with heat, Lea gasped, blinking at them both.

Their matching serious expressions of earnestness melted to smiles. Andy let his hand slide up along the bottom of her breast to where the nipple was now threatening to burst through the fabric, while Sean went back to kissing her hip, his eyes still raised to hers, his hand drifting up the inside of her knee….

"Lock… door?" Lea managed to splutter.

"Already locked," Andy said as his fingers began lightly to tease her nipple through the damned bra and the damned sweater and...

"And nobody else's coming in here until midnight," mumbled Sean into her skirt as *his* fingers slid up beneath the hem, blazing a path of glory up the inside of her thigh.

"Oh," sighed Lea, feeling as if it were a miracle that she was still standing, "Great..."

At that moment, Sean's fingers brushed along the length of her pussy through her panties while Andy pinched her nipple between his thumb and forefinger and — not coincidentally — brought Lea herself to her knees.

Sean gave her a lazy smirk. "Nice of you to join us, Miss Lea."

She couldn't think of any response in that moment other than to stroke their coat-clad chests.

"I think we might be a mite overdressed for this next bit," Andy chuckled.

"Let me undress you both. I've always wanted..." Running her hands down to their crotches, she felt suddenly shy. Overwhelmed.

"Wanted to jump a fireman in his gear?" asked Andy, a smirk still coloring his voice. His fingers continued to tantalize her breasts.

Lea nodded, pushing their coats off their near shoulders.

"Sorry we can't do this with you on a truck," said Sean.

"Fuck the truck," panted Lea, pulling the heavy coats down so that they slid off of the men's arms and onto the floor behind them. She pulled the near suspenders off, then pushed the far ones.

Her fingers trailed down their chests — both vibrating at her her touch — and came to rest on waistbands of their thick trousers. She couldn't see any fly or buttons. "Huh. Am I supposed to *tear* these off?"

"Uh," gasped Andy.

"Velcro," grunted Sean.

"Oohhh." Letting her fingers slide across the fronts of the pants — which were growing visibly tighter — Lea found the closed-away flaps. "Don't want to let go of either of you," Lea sighed. "So how am I going to open these pants? *Stop.*"

Each of the boys had begun to reach for his own fly, but Lea wanted no help. Grinning at them both, she leaned forward and gave the lump at the front of Sean's pants a gentle bite.

Sean sounded as if he might be choking.

But Andy was the less patient of her two men, Lea knew that, and so she turned toward his crotch, grabbed the waistband, and ripped the Velcro flap loose with her teeth. Gazing up into his eyes, she found his zipper with her teeth and pulled it slowly down over her lover's burgeoning erection.

All the while, she kept a firm grasp on the tented front of Sean's trousers.

"Fuck. Lea." Andy's molasses-dark eyes were half-lidded, smoldering.

Her gaze still locked on Andy's, Lea bit his boxers — being careful not to bite *him* (not too hard, at least) — and pulled them and the pants down to his knees on the floor. She kissed her way back up, grabbed his cock, and gave the head a long lick and a kiss.

Andy groaned gratifyingly.

Sean whimpered, and so Lea gave Andy's cock another quick lick, and then turned to her other lover and repeated the entire procedure, her hand stroking Andy's cock to keep it from feeling jealous.

"You want me to suck you?" Lea felt incredibly hot, incredibly powerful — two beautiful hard-ons in her hands, two beautiful mean nodding eagerly at her. "But who first?" she said with a pout — and then a thought came back to her — an incredibly nasty thought from earlier — and she went with it, not wanting to give them or her the room to get nervous: she pulled the two of them so that their balls were pressed together, their cocks a single spear of flesh in her hands. "Mmm," she said, and opened wide, taking both of them into her mouth at once.

Both men began to swear, and that heat, that power, flared even brighter inside of Lea.

She was amazed at how well their cocks fit together — Andy's reverse curve matching Sean's more typical one perfectly. The feeling of those two thick cock pressing over her tongue and into her throat was intoxicating — but almost too much. She backed off of them, just to make sure could still breathe.

Each of her men had grasped the other. Their heads were on each other's shoulder, their eyes closed. It was, Lea thought, the most sublime thing she had ever seen.

As Lea readied herself to take them back into her mouth, Sean began to rock his hips, pressing his cock through her grasp and along Andy's erection.

Andy gasped, "Damn!" He began to rock in opposition to Sean's thrusts.

If Lea had thought that her excitement couldn't grow any further, she'd been wrong. "That... feel good, guys?"

"Fuck, yes," murmured Sean. Pre-cum was spilling from the tip of his cock onto Andy's and onto Lea's hands.

"It's called —" She licked to the two erections into her mouth again. "— frotting."

"Huh," grunted Sean.

"Say what?" muttered Andy, one hand in Lea's hair, the other pulling Sean closer.

"*Frotting.*" A term she'd learned from fanfiction. All those years of reading Gundam Wing and Harry Potter slash had paid off after all! "Two girls rubbing their pussies together, it's called *tribbing.*"

Sean just repeated, "Huh."

Andy, however, opened his eyes again. "T-tribbing?"

"Uh-huh."

"Damn."

Lea took them both into her mouth again, evoking a pair of deep moans before she pulled off again and looked up. "You guys happy? 'Cause I'm pretty fucking happy."

Sean sighed, "Happy, yeah, but…"

"But… we'd kinda like to both wanna be…" Andy hissed as Lea sucked them both in again.

Sean continued, "Inside. You. *Please.*"

"Well," she laughed, "since you ask so politely, how can I refuse!" Letting go of Andy, she moved Sean back a bit, bent down and took him into her mouth.

Andy did as she knew he would: he moved behind her, flipped her skirt up, and gave her pussy a searing kiss.

Lea groaned around Sean's cock, and both men laughed. "Yeah," Andy said, kissing his way up her bottom, "she's got a lot to say when it's her at the receiving end!"

Lea was about to pull off Sean, turn around, and give Andy a piece of what was left her mind when Andy thrust into her, and she didn't have any pieces to spare.

*Perfect.*

There was something about being with Sean and Andy that was just *perfect.* Didn't matter who was filling her mouth and who her pussy, or how well she knew them, or if both were in her hands or between her breasts or…

Sean reached down and cupped Lea's still-covered breasts, which were swaying wildly to Andy's thrusts. His fingers closed around her nipples and…

Mr. Sanderson, her senior-year Composition teacher had spent an entire class period once talking about how some adjectives can't be modified. *A bit pregnant. Really unique.*

*More perfect* — Mr. Sanderson had pointed up at the poster with the preamble of the US Constitution when he said that.

But Lea now felt she had reason to disagree. Before had been *perfect.* Now was *more perfect.* And then Andy's hands slipped around her hip and closed and her clit and…

*Most perfect.*

• • •

Sean and Andy were lying on the floor, each with his head at the other's knees. Lea was draped across them, her top and bra up under her armpits, her skirt around her waist. *Take that, 50 Shades Lady! Bet you didn't see* this *coming!*

Lea giggled moistly and then blinked. "Oh. Fuck. My luggage."

Both men laughed, literally rocking Lea's world. Andy snorted, "Knew we forgot something!"

Before Lea could jump up, Sean slid his hand — which had been resting on her thigh — up to her snatch, stilling her quite effectively. "Told you, Lea. We needed you to identify something."

Blinking, Lea looked at Sean and then at Andy, who laughed again and pointed over by the door. Her well-traveled back-pack and duffel bag were right there. "Oh. Thanks." She grabbed two semi-hard cocks and squeezed them, getting two rumbling groans for her trouble. "And thanks for meeting me."

"We couldn't stay away," said Andy.

Sean added, "And we didn't want you to have to drive with the roads like this." He stroked her hair. "If you don't mind, we get off shift at midnight."

"Mind? Hell, no!"

"Lea," said Sean, his fingertip running along her earlobe, the line of her chin, "You seemed a mite antsy. Is this really okay?"

She was going to answer *Are you fucking kidding?* But she recognized that it was a real question and deserved a real answer. "Yeah. Yeah. It's just…" She kissed Sean's hand and then turned and pulled Andy's to her lips. "I think this all scares me a bit. I mean, I barely know you guys, but this just feels so… *right*. You know?"

"Yeah," Andy said, as both men let their fingers explore her collarbones, her ribs. "Yeah, I reckon we sure as hell know."

"Indeed we do," said Sean. His fingers grazed the bottom of Lea's right breast so that she could *just* feel it. "And we know that worrying about it won't get us nowhere. Now what do y'all both say," he continued in his low, rolling drawl, "about seeing just how *right* we can keep this feeling before Andy and me have to get back out there in the cold?"

Andy and Lea both concurred that Sean's was a mighty good plan.

*Perfect*, even.

# The Visitor Goes to Work

Lea's phone went off, crooning U2 at her.

First day of work.

Meeting with her boss, Sassy.

Meeting with Bob, the theater's artistic director.

Meeting with the box office staff and training on the ticket software with Zach, the theater's resident computer guy.

Tour with Gus, the tech director.

Lea needed to pee.

Heart racing, adrenaline singing through her veins, Lea leapt out of bed to go to the bathroom.

Well. She tried to leap.

Something heavy was holding her down.

Two somethings, in fact: Sean and Andy, whose legs and massive arms wrapped Lea in a cocoon that would have been incredibly sweet if she didn't need to get up and get ready for her first day on the job.

Also, she still needed to pee. "Guys?"

As Bono continued his ode to the glory of the day, Lea's boys snored on.

"Sean? Andy?" Wriggling, Lea realized that her hands were at each of their crotches. What a surprise. She squeezed two well-worn, well-earned morning hard-ons evoking two somnolent groans. "Boys. Get off of me or I'll fry these up for breakfast."

Andy's head shot up. "Uh. 'Morning."

Sean's face rolled off of Lea's right tit. "Hey."

Anxious as she was, Lea couldn't help but smile down at the shit-ton of male gorgeousness that she had somehow managed to snag for herself. "Hey, yourself. I need to get up."

Now Sean sat up. "Right. First day at the theater." He pronounced it as a three-syllable word: *the-AY-tuh*.

"Uh-huh. And as much as I'd love to stay and play — "

"No," both men said, and like the firemen they were sprang out of the bed, treating her to the sight of her shit-ton of pulchritude standing naked and cum-stained on either side of her bed, and making Lea briefly wonder if she *really* needed to be on time for her first day of work....

"We'll start some breakfast," Sean said, pulling on the pajama pants they somehow always put on but somehow never kept on.

Andy reached out to Lea. "You take a shower." When he pulled her up out of bed, momentum carried her body against his, and the feeling tempted Lea to stay.... He gently propelled her toward the bathroom. "You go. I'd say make yourself prettier, but t'ain't possible."

She beamed at him. "Flatterer."

From the kitchen, Sean called, "No, ma'am. Just the facts, ma'am."

"Uh-huh," said Lea with a very non-Southern smirk. "I've got my eye on you two. Don't think I don't."

"No, ma'am," answered Sean, his smile very Southern, and very wicked.

• • •

Standing under the spray, Lea contemplated the fact that tonight would be her first night alone in the apartment. Both of her boys would be back to the firehouse tonight, and that knowledge filled her with anticipated ache, even as it filled her with a bit of relief. Since Andy and Sean had met her at the airport three nights before, it felt as if most of her waking time had been spent in a fog of sexual satiation. One, the other, or both of the boys always seemed to be ready and raring to go, and that was hardly something Lea was going to complain about. Even so, Lea had lost count of the orgasms they'd brought her too, and she hadn't even tried to count the number of times they'd come on or inside of her. Her pussy. Her mouth. Between her tits...

The previous night, when she'd needed to catch her breath, on each other: frotting — grinding their cocks together, each grabbing the other's ass, pulling the other close, Sean on top, Andy with his head pressed against Sean's sweaty shoulder, his eyes locked on Lea's as he bucked against his friend and spurted up against Sean's flat stomach, setting Sean off....

It was just about the sexiest thing that Lea had ever seen, and was the closest she'd ever come to understanding her friend Kirsten's fascination with gay porn.

As the shower poured down on her, Lea felt her nipples hardening, felt the hot water streaming between her labia. *Oh, god....*

Sliding into the corner of the shower stall, trying not to think about time, Lea rubbed her hands over her wet body. She let her fingers trail down between her legs, and hissed as they encountered her pussy — satiated, yes; tired, perhaps; but still ready for more....

"You need a hand there, Miss Lea?"

Through the steam-fogged glass door, Lea could see that Andy and Sean were standing at the door of the bathroom. "Huh," grunted Lea. Bulges in their low-slung pajama pants made it obvious that they were having as hard a time as Lea was *not* thinking about about the last few days. "Uh-huh," she groaned. "*Please.*"

They dropped trou — *why did they ever bother putting them on?* — and stepped into the shower. The brief flash of cool air that they'd let in was immediately replaced by the heat of their bodies pressing against hers.

"Rolls in the oven," mumbled Andy, huge hands flowing over Lea's belly and hips. He leaned down and sucked Lea's right nipple into his mouth, eliciting a spark of pleasure and a small scream.

Sean stopped her mouth — gently, always gently — and began to slowly kiss his way across her cheek to her chin. Up her chin tortuously to her ear. He pulled on her earlobe with his lips, let it slide by the smallest possible degrees out of his mouth, and then whispered, "What you thinking about, Lea? What got you all hot and — " He let his fingers join Andy's sliding along the slick outer lips of her pussy. "— ready for us?"

Whimpering, Lea tried to spread her legs, to open to them, but their massive thighs pressed against hers, and so she settled for letting each run his hand in the crease between either thigh and her pussy. It made Lea wonder why she hadn't ever tried masturbating two-handed.

Would she ever need to masturbate ever again? "Thinking… of you," she groaned as Sean began to apply his amazingly talented, *slow* mouth to her free breast. She reached down, taking two wet hardons into fingers that she could barely control. "Rubbing… 'gainst each other. *Fuck!*"

Sean had finally sucked her left nipple between his teeth.

Into right breast, Andy murmured, "Wouldn't you rather have us rubbin' 'gainst you?"

"Um…" Honestly, Lea had no ability to say what she'd *rather* have, but yes: that sounded very nice indeed. "Uh-huh.…"

Grinning, Sean slid up Lea's body and turned her toward him. Andy pressed up against her back and reached around her, pulling Sean's ass, so that Sean's cock slid up along Lea's belly.

Sean pulled Andy close as well, and his cock slid against the length of her spine, his balls spreading her butt cheeks. Both men began to kiss and nibble at her neck, her cheeks, and to grind aganist her.

*Fuckity-fuck-fuck.*

They were fucking *through* Lea. Lea *was* the fuck. Her entire body felt like one enormous erogenous zone.

Each began to grunt ferally into one of Lea's ears.

*FUCK....*

*But...*

But as exciting as it was — and it was — Lea was aware of her own pussy weeping with need, the greedy thing, adding more moisture to the wet shower. "Um..." She found one leg sliding up onto Sean's hip.

Without any further prompting, Sean's hands slid to Lea's ass and lifted her, so that his cock was grinding against her clit and Andy's was sliding up the crack of her ass. "Damn," he grunted.

"Uh-huh," Lea sighed as the two erections sparked all sorts of fascinating sensations in her lower body.

"Damn," echoed Andy.

The two of them continued their steady rhythm. Lea hardly had do a thing other than enjoy herself and try not to pass out.

After a few minutes she felt the rhythm shift, speeding up. "Uh, Lea, honey?" moaned Sean. "Can I... inside you?"

*"Please!"*

In rhythm, he lifted her, then lowered her onto his cock.

Lea and Sean both swore in some Stone Age language that bore no particular resemblance to English. The feeling of Sean's sweet erection stroking her g-spot as Andy pushed against her pelvis, made her clit grind into Sean's pubic bone...

"Um, Lea? Baby?" Andy whined.

Lea threw back her head and kissed him. "Huh?"

Andy slowed, his expression pained. "Could I maybe...?"

"Oh. Sure. After Sean. I'd... *HNGH*... love... that." Sean had latched onto one of Lea's nipples again.

"Um, yeah, me too, um..." Andy panted, grinding against Lea's ass as Sean thrust up into her cunt. "Uh, maybe...?" He slipped one hand free and steadied his cock, lining it up with Lea's backside.

*"Woah!"* gasped Lea, her buttocks clenching around his head, her body stiffening, her cunt contracting so that Sean screamed his orgasm into her chest, and they all nearly toppled over.

"Sorry!" moaned Andy as Sean slid slowly to the shower floor, Lea on top of him. "I didn't — !"

"No, no, no, it's okay, I mean," panted Lea as she felt Sean pulsing inside of her as she lay on his chest, "I mean maybe we can do that, can talk about that, but, um, not right now, okay?"

"Okay." Andy sounded about five years old.

Sean slid his cock out of Lea, making her gasp again. "Don't worry, Andy. I think sweet Miss Lea here still needs some help gettin' off, and seems to me she's got a very sweet, very hot hole to file."

Lea tilted her pelvis so that Andy could see her pussy, washed by the shower spray, dripping Sean's spray, open to him.

"O-okay." Andy knelt behind Lea, between Sean's thighs, and buried his reverse-curved cock in her, and it was his turn to join her in screaming that Paleolithic war cry.

As Andy began to pound her from behind (and from his whimpers, he was clearly close, which was probably why he'd been so eager to stick his *thang* up her ass, the poor dear, and *oooo*, she was *sooo* close too), Sean's fingers slipped down Lea's belly and through her bush, finding her clit, and...

And...

•••

As the mist cleared, Lea was first aware of *wet*. Wet Sean against her belly. Wet Andy gushing wet inside of her. Wet her. Wet air. Wet tile.

Tears. Water.

*Wet.*

"Think those rolls are done, Andy-boy?" asked Sean, reaching beneath Lea's overflowing pussy and squeezing his friend's balls, releasing more *wet* inside of Lea.

"Aw, *fuck yeah*," groaned Andy.

"Then let's go get this girl fed and off to her new job."

"Fuck yeah," panted Lea with a slack grin. "I'm definitely ready now."

•••

Lea's first day was a whirlwind. Sassy, Lea's sardonic, Canada-born boss, was overjoyed to have a fulltime assistant for the first time in years, and showed Lea off around the office like a new baby. The theater was in the middle of producing one season and mounting its subscription drive for the next one, and so between the main office, the shop, and the box office, there were well over a hundred new faces and new names for Lea to learn. After her last job, where she and the artistic director had comprised the entire fulltime staff, the flood of new people and energy overwhelmed Lea, even as it thrilled her.

Everyone seemed incredibly friendly. She got five different offers of places to stay, and was asked out on three dates — two very different men and one woman — the office manager, Jaimie, who reminded Lea strongly of Sean's sister, Kirsten. It was quite nice to be able to say that she was all taken care of in both regards.

Nicer to be able to say it while she could still feel the remnants of Andy and Sean's passion inside of her.

After watching a few rounds of this, Sassy got an incredibly knowing, wicked look on her face. As they ate lunch in Lea's tiny new office (barbecued ribs, of course, which Sassy claimed was her main reason for staying in Atlanta), Sassy waited until Lea's mouth was full and shot her a sly grin. "So. Boyfriend? Girlfriend?"

"Um," said Lea, trying to swallow, trying to think how to answer. "It's... complicated."

Sassy's eyebrows shot up. "Is it, really? Well, well, well. It's always the quiet ones."

Lea knew she was turning the color of the barbecue sauce, so she didn't even try to answer, letting Sassy chuckle to her heart's content.

As they finished up their lunch, Sassy said, "Complicated is what we do best, of course, but if it becomes *too* complicated, don't feel shy about letting me know, eh?"

"Thanks," said Lea, trying to match Sassy's no-nonsense tone. "I think for now it's just complicated enough."

"Lucky you." Sassy's grin widened. "So, after your last meeting, I'd love to take you out to dinner with Bob." The artistic director of the theater. "Won't be stepping on any plans?"

"No," said Lea. "I'm on my own this evening anyway."

"Oh?" Sassy raised her eyebrow again, but apparently decided to move on. "Well, you've got a training session in the box office with Zach. He's sweet, but watch his hands."

"Okay," said Lea, thinking, *I'd rather watch Sean and Andy's hands, stroking each other...* Smiling, she shook her head, and then remembered her last meeting of the day. "No problem. Do I need to worry about Gus?"

"Oh, no." Sassy gave what was for her a soft, warm smile. "Gus is a sweetheart. You won't have any trouble with him."

"Great." Lea gathered up the napkins and sauce-soaked bags. "Well, let me strap on my armor and go get trained by Zach."

• • •

Zach turned out to be no problem. Lea short-circuited any potential ass-grabbing when she breezed into the box office and asked if he knew where Sean and Andy's firehouse was. "My boyfriend works there," she sighed, "and I'd love to drop in by surprise when I get off work tonight."

Politely Southern as most of the staff, Zach pulled up a map and showed Lea that the firehouse was only a half mile from the theater — which Lea already knew. After Lea had gone on about how wonderful her boyfriend was — and he was, whichever of them she happened to mean — she thanked Zach fulsomely.

He smiled back, a nervous, thin-lipped smile, and proceeded to teach Lea the intricacies of the box-office software.

Zach never touched her.

•••

As Lea walked through the door that led backstage to the domain of Gus, the theater's tech director and senior designer, Lea texted the boys: *Miss me?*

*Like crazy,* came back Andy's immediate answer.

*Think we're both addicted,* added Sean.

Lea shivered and smiled. *Me too. Hey, I'm having dinner with my bosses tonight. Any chance I can swing by and visit after?*

After a minute or so, Sean's answer came back: *Afraid that's probably not a good idea. We kind of pushed our luck swapping shifts to meet you out at the airport. Another time?*

With a sigh, Lea sent them a frownie face, and then texted, *I'll be so lonely in that big pullout without both of you.*

She got two frownie faces in return. *See you tomorrow,* they both answered.

"Ah, Lea, how nice to meet you." Gus was grey-haired and small — pixyish, even — and though he was easily the oldest person working at the theater, his eyes and smile were bright and he was bouncing on the balls of his feet as he approached. "Sally's said such wonderful things about you."

"Glad to hear it!" Lea laughed. "You're the first person I've met here who doesn't call her Sassy."

"Oh, well..." He blinked at Lea. "My wife was named Sally, you know. My late wife."

"Oh." Lea felt all of the heat that had flooded into her middle as she texted Sean and Andy turn cold. "I'm so sorry."

"Oh, no need," Gus said with a bright, sad smile. "It's been four years, though there are days when it feels as if it was only yesterday. But we had a wonderful life together. Here. I'll show you." He led her into the bowels of the shop area behind the main stage; a group of artists were painting an elaborate starscape on what looked like an old barn door. "Looks gorgeous," said Gus, and the crew looked up. "Everyone, this is our new assistant business manager, Lea."

Lea waved. "The box office staff have already dubbed me *Mini-Sassy*," she laughed

The painters waved and introduced themselves; Lea despaired of remembering any more names, and then Gus tugged on her sleeve. "Come on," he said, "let me bring you up to my aerie." He led Lea up a steep staircase — almost more of a ladder — up to a room that was sixty feet or sp above the shop floor.

"Whew!" Lea said when they reached the top. "No wonder you have so much energy! You climb that all of the time?"

"Oh, yes," Gus said, blinking, as if it had never occurred to him that it might be a difficult climb. "I suppose that's why I don't get too many visitors." He flashed his bright smile and ushered Lea in.

The office was easily three times the size of Lea's, but it didn't feel it. It was crammed with set models, blue prints, a wide-format printer, three work tables overflowing with sketches, swatches, paint chips and random pieces of hardware. And the walls were invisible, covered by dozens of brightly colored paintings. A number were of dogs and sailboats, but a number were amazing, impressionistic portraits of actors and...

"Here's my Sally," said Gus, that sad smile resurfacing. Behind what seemed to be his desk — it was difficult to tell, given the glaciers of beautiful bric-a-brac piled on top — hung eight different paintings that featured a beautiful redheaded woman. Well, it was difficult to tell what she *looked* like, but the paintings made it very clear how the painter had *felt* about her. "We were married over forty years," Gus sighed, "and she was as beautiful when I lost her — " He pointed to the portrait furthest to the right, which showed her red hair shot with white. " — as she was when I met her." He pointed at the painting at the opposite end, where her hair seemed to be almost a fire.

"Wow," said Lea, breath truly taken away. She gazed at the other paintings, each stunning, and noticed in three or four another figure: a tall, dark-haired man. "That's not *you*, is it? Do you have a son?"

"Hmm?" Gus followed Lea's gaze. "Oh. No. We didn't have children. That's Frank." Gus's eyebrows bunched, which looked almost unnatural on his face. "He was our friend. Good friend. Well, he was our boarder."

"Boarder?"

"Yes. He lived with us for nearly a quarter century, if you can believe that." Gus sighed. "We lost him nearly a decade ago."

"Oh, Gus, I'm so sorry." Lea felt as if she were walking through a minefield and tripping every last one.

"No, no, don't be, my dear." Gus's eyes were sparkling again, and his mouth was back in its usual bright smile. "One of the things about reaching my age — I'm seventy-eight — is that one loses people. Careless, I know, but it can't be helped! And in the mean time, I've known more than my share of love and laughter, and I've still got work that I enjoy, and a building full of young, creative people keeping me alive. I haven't any complaints!"

• • •

When Lea met up with Bob and Sassy, she was still laughing. "You told me Gus was a sweetheart, Sassy, but *wow!*"

"He's something, eh?" said Sassy with a wink. "I'm convinced he'll be here, running up and down to his office and giggling like a little gnome long after I'm dead and gone."

"Yeah," laughed Bob. "His crew believes he lives on paint fumes. They call him the Painter of Dorian Grey."

They all laughed at that, and the artistic director continued, "Mind, he's a brilliant designer. As much the reason this theater is still standing as anyone. I don't know how the heck we'd ever get by without him. Which, I hope and trust, we won't have to any time soon!"

"Here, here," Sassy agreed. "Now, Lea, let's get out of this building so we can show you that there is in fact food in

Atlanta aside from fried chicken and barbecue. I know we're a little further away from the ocean than you're used to, but there's a seafood place just a few blocks away that makes some of the best sushi you'll find in the South. And while we ply you with seafood and sake, you can give us your impressions of the theater."

The meal was long. The conversation was fascinating. The sake flowed freely.

And the sushi was definitely fabulous.

*I know Sean would love this place; wonder if I could get Andy here?* Lea imagined their hulking forms in the beautiful, quiet restaurant. She imagined them nibbling at the sushi.

She imagined them under the table, nibbling at *her*, and she blushed.

•••

When she arrived back at the apartment, it was almost eleven, and she was dead on her feet. Happy, but exhausted. She was almost glad that she would be able to fall into bed alone and simply go to sleep.

Almost.

There was a package in front of the door. Addressed to her.

Intrigued, Lea picked it up and let herself in.

The apartment was neat as a proverbial pin. There were roses on the table. A note that read, *We can't keep you warm with our bodies tonight, but we hope our love can help at least a little.* They'd both signed it.

It made Lea's middle go soft and her eyes overflow, and she felt like such a *girl*, but what the fuck: she *was* a girl, proud to be one, and she had more than her share of masculinity at her beck and call (if not tonight) — and they'd been incredibly sweet.

Suddenly, she missed them terribly, even though she knew their purpose in leaving the flowers and the note had been quite the opposite.

She threw herself down into one of the chairs — usually Andy's chair — only then remembering the package.

It was from a store that sounded vaguely familiar, one in San Francisco, but not one that Kirsten had ever worked at, Lea was pretty sure. She couldn't think why it seemed familiar.

Using her keys to cut the packing tape (and trying to ignore the voice of her father telling her not to use her keys that way), Lea opened the box and pulled out the invoice, which included a note from Kirsten: *A housewarming present for my best friend, K.*

Intrigued, she pulled out the newsprint that had been used as packing material — reminding herself to ask the boys where to find a recycling center. In the box were several smaller boxes and a tangle of nylon, plastic, and fabric that, as Lea pulled it out, looked like some bizarre combination of sports gear and lingerie. *What the fuck, Kirsten?*

She lay aside the whatever-it-was, and pulled out the smallest of the boxes. It contained what looked like nothing more than a plastic plumb bob, about three inches long, with a strawberry-shaped head. It was colored bright purple.

Alarmed now, Lea grabbed the largest box, having some sense of what it would contain — and it did.

A penis. Not quite as long as Sean's or Andy's, but a very nice size, to Lea's eye. Made out of silicone.

It too was bright purple. And had what looked like a handle at the back end.

Lea had her phone out and had hit her friend's number before she could even think to breathe.

"Hey, Leelee!" Kirsten's voice was warm, and bright, and welcome. "You get my package, sweetie?"

*"Holy fuck, Kirsten!"* Lea gasped. "What the fuck am I supposed to *do* with this?"

"Well, now, Lea, sugar," laughed Kirsten, "I am quite sure that you could figure out something to do with it all on your lonesome. But I kinda figured that with all of that boyflesh around you, there might be some fun uses you could put it too!"

*"Kirsten!"* Lea felt about thirteen, felt about as humiliated as she had when she figured out why the boys sometimes walked

with their notebooks in front of their crotches. "I mean, thanks a lot, but I've got to tell you, I may be alone tonight, so I'm sure it will be great, thanks, but I've got two very nice penises already — your *brother's* being one! — so I don't see how having yet another phallus to stick inside of me is going to do me a whole lot of good!"

Kirsten cackled. "Oh, I know it'll do you a *whole* lotta good!" She laughed again and then said, "But Lea sweetie, that isn't just for you, you know!"

"Isn't just...?" Lea puzzled at the floppy plastic thing. "It's a dildo, for fuck's sake. I know what a dildo is."

Again Kirsten laughed maniacly. "And what do you think that doodad at the bottom is for?"

Lea grabbed it. "I don't know, a handle?" When Kirsten snorted, Lea growled, "*Kirsten!*"

"Heh! Okay. Okay. Well, did you try on the harness?"

"What, the nylon thing? I'm supposed to *wear* it?"

"Definitely," Kirsten said with a giggle, and before Lea could bark at her again, Kirsten asked, "You in pants or a dress, or what?"

Lea blinked, disconcerted. "Dress. It was my first day."

"Perfect. So slip that nylon thingee on like it was undies. You can slip off what you got or not, whatever."

Perplexed, Lea did as she was told; letting her panties fall to the floor, she stepped into what she could now clearly see were loops for her legs. "Okay."

"Really? Damn, I didn't think it would be that easy."

"Kirsten."

"Sorry. Yeah. So it's not all the way up, is it?"

"Nope." Lea had pulled it to just above her knees.

"Perfect. Now, see at the front, there's a kind of plastic ring, goes right over where your bush would be? Take the dong and slide it through there."

Lea did — and comprehension began to dawn. But still... "But... where will the handle go?"

Kirsten snorted again, but swallowed it. "Sorry! But that's not a handle."

"Not a...?" Lea pulled the harness up the rest of the way, trying to see how the whole thing would work.

As soon as she had pulled it the whole way up, the purple hard-on sprang proudly in front of her, and the protuberance that she'd taken for a handle pushed up against her entrance. *"Oh!"* As soon as Lea's body began to react to the pressure, it slid in. *"OH!"*

"It's called a double dildo, sweetie. A strap-on." Kirsten sounded very pleased with herself. "You ever wonder what it would feel like to fuck your guy, to have a cock? Well, now you have one!"

As the smaller end of the dildo pushed up into Lea's pussy, a nub at the front began pressing against her clit. Grasping the purple phallus with her free hand, she rocked her hips and felt the nub moving against her, the smaller phallus moving within her. "Oh..." she sighed.

"Uh-huh," said Kirsten. "Told you. Feel good?"

"Um. Yeah." Lea and Kirsten had talked about sex a lot, had even discussed vibrators a few times, but they'd never actually talked while *doing it* and Lea was feeling more than a bit uncomfortable — all the more so since she knew that Kirsten was even more bisexual than her brother Sean and had had a crush on Lea. "But, um, what am... How...?"

"Well, me," Kirsten said, all but purring now, "I like to do Gianna with it, right?"

"Sure, but — "

*"But* , see, there's *ways* to use it with a guy too. You see the butt plug?"

"Huh?"

"Thang looks like a big ol' strawberry? And there should be a bottle of lube in there, and a DVD."

Lea stared at the plumb bob. *Butt plug?* Still more than a little distracted by the feeling of the dildo inside of her, she searched the box; indeed, there was a small bottle of lube and a DVD. *"Guide to... Pegging?"*

"Yup. Peggin'. Trust me on this: Guys like gettin' it almost as much as they like givin' it." Now Kirsten was most definitely purring. "God, what I wouldn't give to see you take big ol' country-boy Andy up the ass."

"Huh."

"But Lea, sweetie?"

"Huh?"

"I don't want to know what you and my brother get up to, okay?"

"Uh... 'Kay."

"Now, tell me, sweetie! How was your first day?"

Lea gave Kirsten the full rundown — though her mind was definitely occupied.

•••

After her best-friend-forever hung up ("Gotta go use *my* srap-on on my girlfriend!"), Leah watched the video.

She was with Kirsten on this one. *Lea* wanted to see herself fuck Andy's sweet ass. And Sean's.

After the video was over, she brought all of her new toys into the bathroom, still wearing her harness and dildo, which she couldn't bring herself to take off.

She opened the lube and spread some over the butt plug, and then put a dollop on her finger and distributed it gently to the inside of her anus. Her *asshole*.

And then she slid the butt plug gently in.

She had tried anal sex with a couple of her boyfriends — well, they had tried it with *her.* It sure hadn't been her idea.

It hadn't been a whole lot of fun. But then neither of them had known what the fuck they were doing. John the Controlling Asshole had considered lube to be a sign of decadence. There wasn't any burning feeling now. Just a feeling of fullness, of *nastiness,* like saying forbidden words when she was a kid or touching her first boyfriend Sam's cock.

And feeling both of her lower openings spread, even as her clit was beginning to vibrate against the little nub... *Lordy-lord-lord.*

Lea stared at the purple penis in the mirror, holding up the front of her dress. What was it that was so fucking sexy about it?

But it was.

Having poured a little more lube onto her hand, she grabbed the dildo and began to rock her hips, thrusting the faux cock through her fingers — just *practicing*, to see what it would feel like.

It felt... weird. Good. Weird. The little dildo inside of her created a really nice sense of friction and of pressure. She was aware of her butt being spread every time she thust forward through her fist and clenched her ass cheeks — still, it didn't hurt at all, it felt good, but... weird.

The closest thing Lea could think of was the time that John had taken her out to dinner with a mini-egg vibe inside of her, and the control on his keychain.

Only this time, she was in control.

Did it feel like this for the boys when they jerked off? Well, she thought, it almost certainly felt even better. That being the case, she couldn't believe that they could manage to keep their hands off of themselves at all.

Her boys...

Watching through the mirror as her purple cock thrust through her slick fingers, Lea could feel her nerves beginning to catch fire — the little mini-dildo inside of her was rubbing her g-spot, the nub was rubbing her clit, and the butt plug in her ass and the dildo in her hand had her feeling *so* fucking sexy....

Her boys. Standing almost right here. Watching her in the shower. Getting hard. Rubbing themselves. Fucking *through* her. *Oh. Oh. Ooooohhh....*

The orgasm wasn't titanic, but it shook her — nipples buzzing, vaginal muscles, ass muscles, legs quivering spastically.

She collapsed, panting, against the counter.

Without even thinking, Lea took out her phone. She snapped one picture of the dildo in the mirror, her legs spread,

the silicone glistening. Then she turned around and lifted the
the back of her dress and took a picture of the little purple
hexagon spreading the cheeks of her ass.

Before she could chicken out, she texted the pictures to
Sean and Andy.

And waited.

A minute later, Andy texted back, *WTF?*

Sean texted, *Video chat?*

*You someplace private?* Lea asked, knowing they were on duty.
*Privateish.*

*Okay. I'll go get my laptop. Text when you're ready.*
*Okay.*

Lea considered taking the strap-on off and removing the
butt plug, but no — visual aids were always good for educational
presentations. And they'd clearly gotten the boys' attention.

And so she walked out into the living room, the silicone
dick wobbling in front of her, her ass muscles squeezing around
the plug, feeling incredibly silly and incredibly sexy, both a the
same time.

She set up her laptop on her bed and knelt, waiting for Sean
and Andy to get online.

She didn't have to wait long.

"Hey, Lea." They were crowded together in a small, dark
space.

"Hello, boys. Where the hell are you?"

"Um. Cab of the ladder truck," said Andy sheepishly.

Sean gave an embarrassed smirk. "Biggest closed space we
could find away from the bunks."

Before Lea could answer, Andy said, "But hey, Lea-sugar,
how was your first day?"

"Oh! Great!" And Lea told them about her day from beginning to end, only vaguely aware that she was stroking the dildo
in her hand or rocking against the one in her pussy.

She didn't tell them about Gus's paintings. It seemed...
personal. Intimate, though she wasn't sure why.

They *ooo*'d and *aaah*'d in all of the right places, promised to beat up Zach if she wanted, and then, when she was done, fell silent.

After a moment, Andy said, "So. Lea."

"Hmm?"

His expression was serious. "What the ever-loving *fuck* were those pictures you sent?"

"Didn't you like them?"

Sean answered, "Well, Lea, sweetheart, *like* isn't quite the word. *Nearly had to perform CPR on each other* is closer to it."

"Mmm," purred Lea. "Would have liked to see that."

"Uh-huh," Sean answered. "So...?"

"Well," Lea answered, aware that her voice was a bit higher than usual, "I got some toys for us to play with and I just wanted to show you." She thought that mentioning that she'd gotten them from *Kirsten* probably wouldn't make her brother very comfortable.

"Toys?" gulped Andy.

"Uh-huh." She got up on her knees so that they could see the dildo and the harness. "This lovely strap-on, and — " She turned around and lifted her dress. " — this lovely butt plug. And a very educational video that taught me *all sorts* of interesting things that we could do with them. And I've been playing with them all by myself tonight, which is nice, but I thought, perhaps, we could play with them together."

Sean licked his lips. "Uh-huh."

Andy seemed to be sweating. "To... Together?" Andy jumped and caught his breath, and Lea was pretty sure that Sean had grabbed Andy's crotch.

Lea sighed. "Yeah. Together. See, the thing is, Andy, you asked if I would take you up my ass this morning, and, you know, I want to, because the idea of both of you inside of me at the same time is fucking amazing, but it's also kind of scary, you know? But I do want to give you that, because I love you both so much."

Both men gulped but nodded. "Love you too."

Lea felt heat spread through her whole body, and knew that it wasn't a blush of embarrassment or shame. "So, here's my bargain: if you want me to take it up the ass, I would love to, but you have to agree to take it up the ass as well."

"Jesus, baby," said Sean.

"Let *you* take us up the, um, ass," asked Andy, eyes wide, "or take, you know...?"

Sean glanced at his friend. His lover. "Andy?"

Andy's fair skin darkened and he looked down. "Or take, you know... each other?"

"Oh," said Sean.

"Oh, Andy, baby," gasped Lea. "That's... That's up to the two of you." Pulling her dress over her head, Lea smiled. "Now, if you'd like, I can show you some of the things we can do with these toys. Would you like that?"

"Oh, yeah," said Andy, face still dark.

"Please," added Sean, grinning.

And Lea did.

And they did like it.

And so did she. She took great pleasure in the knowledge of a job well done.

# Epilogue: The Visitor Plays for Keeps

It was football season, and so Lea knew where she'd find them — where she *hoped* she'd find them — after she'd finished house-managing the Sunday matinee: watching the game, sitting at the edge of the pullout they all now shared.

Well, *Sean* was sitting.

Andy was kneeling between Sean's thighs sucking at his roommate's long, gorgeous, spotted dick.

*Fuck*, thought Lea, *how the fuck did I get so lucky?* "So, Sean, you win a bet, or lose one?"

Her lover's eyes were half-closed from the pleasure that their other lover was giving him. "Won it. Idiot thought the Falcon's'd score on the last drive."

"Never bet against the San Francisco team, Andy, don't you know that?" laughed Lea, dropping her clothes to the floor and sliding up behind Andy, taking his semi-hard cock in hand, working to make sure that there was nothing *semi* about it. Once it was fully erect, she sidled her way between them.

Andy moaned, and Sean's cock popped free; Lea licked at it even as Andy moved behind her and pushed that wonderful inverted *thang* of his into her weeping pussy. "*Holy fuck,*" she cried into Sean's cock head. Panting, she said, "Now, I hope you boys left some for me?"

They both gasped, "Yes, *ma'am.*"

Swallowing Sean as Andy began to plow her from behind, she thought, *What good boys you are!*

And then thought became unimportant, because the whole fucking world was absolutely fucking *perfect* once more.

As it absolutely fucking always should fucking be.

•••

# Coming Soon: The Visitor Entertains

*Lea treats Andy, Sean — and Sean's mother — a wonderful show at the theater. And the next evening, she provides some very special entertainment of her own.*

# Three for Three

Sometimes, these friends find,
three is just the *right* kind of crowd

# Truth & Games

## Playing a Kids' Game... Adult-Style

"Let's play a game," Felicity said, as Aaron mixed their third round of Margaritas on her kitchen counter. Though it was late spring, it looked like anything but. The rain was coming down in sheets outside. Sheets.

Ben snorted. "What kind of game? Poker? You hate it. Go Fish?"

Felicity pulled one of her curls out so that she could see it, searching for the grey that would appear one of these years. "I had something different in mind," she said.

"What?" Aaron said wryly as he splashed tequila liberally into the pitcher, "Spin the Bottle? Truth or Dare?"

"Something a little more like that, I suppose," said Felicity as demurely as she could manage, reaching down and pulling a tiny clear vial from her purse, which was resting on the floor beneath the table.

"What the hell's that, Lici?" Ben asked. Aaron placed the lime-green pitcher in the center of table and peered at the little bottle, clearly intrigued.

"Truth serum," said Felicity and held up the label. "Amobarbital."

They stared at her. "Felicity," Aaron said, "Isn't that stuff supposed to be strictly controlled...?"

"I do have prescription privileges, you know. Besides, one of the perks of working in a research hospital," said Felicity. "I get to... circumvent some of the control laws from time to time."

"Fuck," Ben muttered. "I always said we were a bad influence on this girl."

She gave them what she hoped was a suitably evil smile.

"So," Aaron said, pouring the drinks out even as his eyes remained fixed on the bottle in Felicity's fingers, "what sort of game was it that you had in mind?"

"Well, first we drink up," Felicity said, carefully titrating three drops into each of the three glasses. Aaron was chewing his lip. Ben looked white as a sheet. "Don't you trust me?" she asked, and downed half of her sour-sweet tumbler.

"Course we do..." Ben muttered and looked to Aaron, who merely shrugged. "Fuck. Cheers."

"Cheers," Aaron said, and they drank, deeply.

As the Margarita hit bottom, Ben gave a shiver, then looked up. "So..."

Both men looked at her expectantly.

"What I have in mind is quite simple. Each of us gets to ask the other two a question — any question, and it has to be the same question for both people. And obviously," she said, raising her drink, "we have to answer honestly."

"Does the person who asks have to answer too?" Ben asked, his fingers drumming on the glass.

"Absolutely," Felicity said, and waited.

Aaron had his serious face on, and Ben's forehead was glistening with a thin sheen of sweat.

"Right," Aaron said, "I'll ask first."

Ben turned to look at his friend as though waiting to be attacked at any moment.

"Okay. Here it is: What's the wildest sexual experience you've ever had?"

Ben let out a bark of either agony or relief.

Felicity found herself talking. "Remember Lisa's bachlorette party? Maybe you don't, you were both out getting poor Connor shit-faced, if I remember. Anyway —"

"Don't tell me you slept with a male stripper!" Ben said, looking thoroughly disapproving.

"No, silly boy, it was your sister. Lisa was really drunk, and after everyone left, I was trying to help her get into my bed, just in the other room there —" Felicity pointed over her shoulder. "— so she could actually make it to her own wedding, when she reaches up and kisses me." In spite of everything, Felicity could feel the heat coming to her cheeks. "It was really weird. I mean, here's my best friend, other than you two, and she was doing things with her tongue that were just —"

"I DON'T WANT TO KNOW!" Ben shouted.

"And when I started to stick my fingers —"

"STOP!"

Ben and Aaron stared down at the drinks. "That stuff is amazing," Aaron muttered.

Ben grunted, looking even paler.

"I think I'm going to go into your bedroom and jack off right there on the bed," Aaron said. "That's the sexiest fucking thing I've ever heard."

"I think I'm going to be sick," Ben said.

"Really?" Felicity asked Aaron, ignoring Ben.

Aaron nodded. "Should I?"

"No," Felicity said, "I want to hear Ben's answer. Ben?"

Ben looked up at her, his face still white. "It was when we went to Anguilla after you finished med school, Lici. A Japanese girl, couldn't understand a thing she said, but it didn't matter. There was this hammock set up right on the beach, and we spent the entire night fucking without once touching the ground. Okay?" he whined.

"Uh, yeah," Aaron said. "Amazing. Let's see. Mine —"

"I don't want to hear it if it was Lisa, okay?" said Ben.

"But she took me up into the attic at your folks' house, Ben

—"

"STOP, PLEASE!"

Aaron leaned over to Felicity and whispered, "She really could do the most amazing things with her mouth, couldn't she?"

Felicity began to giggle, until she saw Ben's miserable face. "Sorry," she said.

"No, you're not," Ben pouted.

"No, you're right, I'm not. You should see your face, Ben. You look absolutely mortified."

"Well, I am. It was bad enough knowing that Aaron used to sleep with my sister. But both of you?" He shook himself like a dog getting out of water, and Aaron and Felicity laughed. "I'll never use that bed in the attic ever again. And I'll never be able to look my sister in the face again."

Felicity began, "It was just the one —"

"STOP," Ben said, very firmly, and Felicity sat, her lips pursed, hands folded on the table before her.

"So," she said, once the urge to giggle had subsided again, "what's your question for us, Ben? I could tell you some things about Seamus… and Scott…" Ben and Lisa's younger brothers, who were also twins.

"Holy fucking hell, woman, is there a member of my family you haven't slept with?"

"Well," she said with a snort, her stomach warming in spite of the cold drinks, "at least it wasn't both of them at the same time. And of course, I've never slept with you." Both their faces contorted, Ben's in deep abashment and Aaron's in a sort of distracted thoughtfulness. "So," she repeated, "what do you want to ask us, Ben?"

"No sexual exploits, thanks a lot. I'll be digesting all of that for years." Some of the old fire flared back into Ben's eyes, making Felicity very warm inside indeed. "Okay, how about this: what's your happiest memory of school?"

They'd met in college, living on the same freshman dorm hallway.

"Wow," Aaron said, tapping the half-empty glass vial against the table, "I'll tell you the truth—choosing one is hard. There's the day we graduated. Couldn't believe we'd survived. Together. Then... Making the traveling squad for the track team. The first few months with Lisa — sorry, Ben," he said. Aaron's on-again-off-again romance with Ben's twin, which had ended finally when Lisa got engaged to their friend Connor, was the longest-standing relationship any of the three of them had had, in college or since. Felicity was happy that the Aaron and Lisa were friends again.

Aaron looked up at the ceiling. "There was a spring day during our senior year, right after I'd won my last race, when I remember just sitting down by the lake with you two, and Lisa and Seamus and Connor."

Ben nodded. Felicity could still smell the cool mossiness of the lake, the spicy scent of the eucalyptus floating across from the other side, the musk of Aaron's sweat. Ben playing his guitar.

"But really," Aaron said, "if I had to pick one, it would be junior year, after Lisa and I broke up the first time. I mean," he smirked, "me and Lisa fighting wasn't fun, but that isn't what I remember. It was after I got spiked at the UCLA meet, and you finally talking to me, Ben. And then you starting to cry, Felicity. And hugging us both. I thought you'd both gone absolutely nuts." He looked at them, his blue eyes flashing. "But I don't think I've ever been happier in my life."

Ben looked up, smiled, and punched Aaron in the shoulder, "Thanks, dude."

"Wow," Felicity murmured. "I was so happy then too. Even if I was crying and you didn't know what to do with me. And Alexei kissing me on the quad, though that doesn't seem like such a happy memory these days. Graduation, yes." Passing bottles of Cold Duck and Dom Perignon back and forth. "Meeting the two of you."

"Meeting us?" Ben crowed. "You came in and asked us what the hell we were doing in your room!"

Felicity blushed. She had miscounted the doors and was

astonished to find that her roommates were apparently two boys: tall, fair Ben and wiry, dark Aaron.

Smirking, Aaron pushed her foot with his. "You all but told us we were useless idiots."

Blushing on, she laughed. "Well, you are useless idiots. But you were also the most beautiful boys I'd ever seen. Wish I'd stayed in your room. Connor wouldn't have minded rooming with Lisa and Jenn."

"God, Felicity," Aaron said, wrinkling his nose, "were you even seventeen yet? You'd never even had a boyfriend or anything, had you?"

She'd always been the youngest of them, though it'd never felt that way. "Well, no. But it's the truth," she replied, lifting her glass. Part of why she'd been so hard on them was that her first reaction to seeing two boys unpacking in what she was certain was her room had been very physical, very positive, and absolutely humiliating. "But the happiest memory? I mean, the happiest memory? It was later freshman year, Halloween. I'd wanted so much for you to like me, both of you, and you'd said all those horrible things about me, Ben — and yes, they were mostly true — but then Rick got me drunk, and the two of you…" Tears began to well up in her eyes. "Sorry. You backed him off, and stayed with me all night while I was throwing up, even though I knew you didn't like me very much…"

"We did like you," Aaron said, "sort of. We just hadn't realized it. And we didn't know what to do with you."

"We still don't," muttered Ben.

Felicity laughed. "It made me realize just who you two were. Not just that you were beautiful. That you were so wonderful, both of you. And so sweet. And funny."

"Funny looking, you mean," chuckled Ben, uncomfortable with sentiment as always.

Felicity shot him a look. "You came and took care of me because it was the right thing to do. That totally changed me."

"Did, didn't it?" Ben mused. He looked up. "You know,

sometimes, I miss the old smartypants —" This time it was Felicity's turn to punch, and she landed a solid blow to his bicep. "Ow! I'm going to need that arm!"

Felicity smirked. "Good thing there's a doctor in the house then."

"Your turn, Ben. What's your happiest memory?" Aaron said quietly, swirling his glass.

"Till a few years ago," Ben said, rubbing his arm, "I would have said it was getting together with Maya. But the pleasure's faded right out of that." He'd pined after Maya for years. Sweet idiot. Ben shook his head and looked at Aaron. "Same as yours, dude. It'd been so hard being angry with you, hanging out with Seamus and Lisa. And being so angry that you'd gone and broken my sister's heart — and yeah, I know she was the one who called it off that time, that she hurt you, but it didn't feel it then. Mad that Her Majesty here wouldn't just take my side. Then watching you bleeding there on the track, and Lici and me climbing into each other's skins, we were so worried. And then it all just didn't matter any more, because you were all right, and you were talking to me again. And," he thrust a thumb towards Felicity, "she went fucking crazy and started weeping all over the two of us." He screwed up his face. "Funny thing to be happy about, you know?"

Aaron nodded, a smile barely painting his mouth. Then he turned back to Felicity. "So, Felicity, your turn. What's your question?"

She felt her stomach flutter. "Well." She looked from one to another, brown eyes and blue eyes focused on her. "The thing is…" But the fluttering bubbled right up into her throat and she couldn't speak. Damn. She was always better at theory than practice.

"Come on, Lici-lick-it," Ben said. "cough it up."

"You must have had a question you wanted to ask, or you wouldn't have dreamed this whole thing up," Aaron said, his gaze like the ocean off the Santa Monica pier that really calm day when Dad had bought her cherry soda, with sugar and everything.

"Felicity. What's your question?"

"Ifyoucouldmarryanyonewhowoulditbe?" The words got out between the flutters, leaving her deflated.

Without a pause, without looking at each other, without blinking, both men answered, "You."

"Hunh."

"That's what I love about Felicity," Ben said. "She's so fucking articulate."

Twin tidal waves seemed to be sloshing up to her throat and down towards the pit of her stomach. Rebounding. Crossing. Rebounding again.

Aaron turned to Ben. "That's why I never could ask her out, you know? Because you..."

Ben nodded, then looked across the table. "C'mon, Felicity." Ben searched her face, very seriously. "Time for you to answer."

"Cards-on-the-table time." Aaron started to reach across to take her hand, but stopped himself. She stared at a point immediately between the two of them. "Felicity, if you could marry anyone in the world, who would it be?"

"You," she sighed to that point on the table. "Both of you. I've loved you both for as long as I've known you. I've wanted you both for... Well, for a very long time." She looked up. "I'd sort of hoped that one or both of you would admit that you have someone else you wanted to spend the rest of your life with. That I'd be spared the impossible task of choosing...."

Felicity stood, teetering — realizing just how drunk and nervous she was. "When I... dreamed this up, I knew you both might answer, you know, the way you did. It seemed so unlikely... But, in my, you know, in my fantasy, at this point..." She took a deep breath, squared her shoulders and looked at the two of them looking up at her. "I'm going right in there, into my bedroom. And I'm going to take off my clothes. And I am going to get into bed." She took another deep breath. "You are both welcome to join me. But only if it's both of you. If one or both of you finds this too... uncomfortable, I will certainly understand. Please lock the door on your way out, and we can pretend this never happened."

With as much dignity as she could muster, she stutter-stepped into her room and closed the door.

When she had fantasized this scene, she had been perfectly in control of her feelings, had treated them to a sultry retreat and a wink. Now however she was so terrified by what she had just said to them that she couldn't open the buttons to her blouse. She stood, fumbling with her own clothes, and cursing.

A low roll of thunder made the hair on Felicity's arms stand on end.

The door opened.

Aaron came in first, followed by Ben, who seemed to be trying to hide behind his friend, and was failing miserably, because of his height.

They were both entirely naked.

"Hunh."

"You said that before, Felicity." Aaron stepped to the side, looking perfectly relaxed, like Michaelangelo's David, except that he wasn't holding a sling and, oh, God, his very hard cock was pointed very emphatically just over Felicity's head. Also, unlike David, Aaron was demonstrably Jewish. He glanced to his side, where Ben was standing, slowly hyperventilating, his long hands over his crotch. "Ben, what are you doing? I've seen you naked before."

"She hasn't," Ben said. With a shamed smirk, he drew away his hands. A long arc of dark pink flesh was poking him in the navel.

Felicity couldn't even manage Hunh.

"So," Ben said, sidling away from Aaron. "Need help with that shirt?"

"Not yet," Felicity blurted, finding her articulators at last. "Just... watch." It wasn't much of a strip show. It wasn't intended to be. She simply needed to find her feet again. Let the oxygen reach her brain again.

Aaron and Ben watched, very attentively.

Deliberately, methodically, she finally undid her blouse and dropped it from her shoulders. The boys stared fixedly at her bra. Well, at what was under the bra, Felicity supposed. Which was gratifying. She was happy that she had given in to impulse and gone for red lace instead of her usual white cotton — she could hear her mother tsking, Such a fuss to clean, Felicity, dear.

The bra followed the blouse to the floor. She could pick them up later. Skirt and panties dropped, and she could feel how wet she was, and how open, and Aaron actually whimpered, standing there.

"So," Ben said, so quietly that his voice almost faded into the sound of the rain against the window, "how are we going to, uh, do this?"

Felicity backed against her bed and sat on the big feather duvet. Reaching for two books on her bedside table, trying to keep the flutters from choking her again, she said, "I've been doing some research —"

Aaron and Ben burst into laughter and leapt onto the bed on either side of her.

Felix, the big black tom cat who had been her only long-term bedmate, yowled his disapproval and strutted out from behind Felicity's mound of pillows with a look of utter disdain on his feline face. Swishing his tail, he withdrew to the kitchen.

Her arms around either neck, Felicity gazed up at her two men. Who to kiss first?

With a strength she didn't know she had, she pressed the two faces together, and then pushed her lips against two open, astonished mouths. For a second, they both pulled against her, but the heat of the kiss pulled them both in, and their hands began to rove, both finding her flowing, flowering vulva at the same magical moment. Someone was groaning. Perhaps it was she.

Lightning flashed. Thunder rumbled.

Aaron broke first, but it was just to stare down at them. His eyes were so deep, and Ben's oak brown and full of flame. Aaron was sea and sky, that was it, and Ben was earth and fire. And that made her...

"I'm the quintessence," she sighed giddily. At least she thought she did, because at that moment, two tongues began to search her breasts, and all ability to speak was gone, and the old question of why humans have two nipples when one will do was answered in Felicity's mind forever.

• • •

For the rest of her life, Felicity would remember that night as an ecstatic blur punctuated by moments of arc-lit, lightning-struck clarity.

The first image — and Felicity was sure that it was the first, because her comforter was still on her bed — was of her thighs splayed over two sets of shoulders, two shocks of hair spraying onto her stomach, and the feeling of two tongues dancing like flame along her open sex. She was sure she was howling, but had no idea what words were coming out of her mouth.

But she could remember the taste of tears in her mouth, sharp and joyous.

The next memory — and Ben was fond of pointing out that he didn't believe that it was actually next, just the one that she and Aaron remembered as next — was lowering herself onto Aaron, feeling the thickness of him swell within her, feeling herself just on the edge of falling into those bottomless eyes. Aaron reaching up and caressing her cheek, nudging it slightly. She turned her head, mouth open, expecting to find Ben's tusk of a penis. Instead it was Ben's lips that met her, and she kissed him. And it was into his eyes that she gazed and into his mouth that she moaned when her cunt pulsed around Aaron's cock.

The image after that — and Ben of course insisted that it had happened first — was of the two boys sitting against her headboard, each stroking his own cock.

What a waste, she thought. "If one of you makes the other come, he can do anything to me that he wants."

Ben looked dubiously down at Aaron's cock, while Aaron

pondered Felicity. "Anything?" Aaron asked.

"Anything," repeated Felicity, opening her legs wide just to emphasize the point.

She knew them well enough to know that they'd do just about anything if it involved friendly competition. What she hadn't expected was how comfortably they reached across and began to stroke each other.

Excited by the spectacle of these two beautiful men — her two beautiful men — happily wanking each other, and unwilling to make it easy on them, Felicity began to slip her middle finger inside herself, and to diddle her swollen clitoris with her thumb.

They both closed their eyes when she slid a second finger in. "Fuck, Lici, have a heart," Ben moaned.

"You two done this before?" Felicity teased.

"Uh," Aaron said. Ben turned scarlet.

"Really?" Felicity squealed, her thumb whirring faster.

"It was just um… once," Aaron panted, a look of intense concentration on his face. "Sophomore year. On Connor's bed. Drunk and horny as all fuck. All… four of us. Seamus. Connor!"

As Aaron had been talking, Ben had swooped down and gulped Aaron's bulbous cockhead into his mouth.

"Shit!" Aaron howled, eyes wide open, as he let go of Ben's penis and grabbed his friend's blond mane. Ben had sucked Aaron into his mouth all of three times before Aaron was screaming again, "Shit, Ben! Oh, God, shit!"

Felicity screamed too, her cunt pulsing around her fingers.

When Ben looked up, he had a triumphant gleam in his eye, and semen sprayed across most of his face. Felicity dove over to him and began cleaning his chin with her tongue. "Can't believe I did that," he said. "Hey, dude, you tell anyone I did that, and I'll tell 'em you enjoyed it!"

The taste of Aaron still bitter and slick on his lips, his tongue, Ben began to kiss Felicity passionately, so that she was fairly certain that Ben didn't hear Aaron say, "I did, actually."

"So," Felicity whispered into Ben's ear, "a deal's a deal. I'm all yours. What do you want?" She could imagine dozens of possibilities that he might suggest, most of which might be great fun, any of which she was actually willing to try in that moment.

His breath heavy in her ear, Ben panted, "I just want to fuck you, Lici. I've wanted to do that for so long…"

And so she lay back on the bed, and wrapped her legs up over Ben's hips while Aaron smiled, winked, and began to play with himself again.

The look on Ben's face would have made Felicity laugh if it hadn't melted her insides at the same time. He was so sweet and so hungry….

He sawed his long, curved prick slowly into her, sending sparks up to the crown of her head. His knees pressed under her hips and they began to roll rhythmically, gently, steadily, his teeth pulling at her neck, her nails pulling at his ass. Floating among the sparks in her brain was the realization that this was why they called it Rock and Roll, and that made her smile.

Somewhere, somehow — how did his head get in there? — Aaron's tongue began swirling around her labia and Ben's balls, which set them both off like Fourth of July rockets.

The rest of the night would become disjoined in her memory, an unplayed puzzle. Her teeth on someone's testicles — Aaron's, most likely. A finger circling her asshole, making her jump and laugh. A tongue passing an oyster-cool dollop of cum onto hers. Passing it along to a different tongue. The candles that she had lit at the four corners of her bed painting everything golden as memory.

She had spent a lifetime hating her body. Her breasts. Her thighs. Her hair. Yet Aaron and Ben adored her. They literally bathed her in desire and love and she felt so beautiful it hurt.

• • •

The last clear image — and she knows it is the last, because the storm had passed and tired morning light was leaking in through the window — was of Ben, flat on his stomach, one hand curled cozy around Aaron's cock, the other resting on Felicity's breast.

"Got a new happiest memory," he muttered. "New wildest experience, too. Love you." And then he let loose a long, rasping snore.

"Love you," Aaron sighed. He was gazing down at Ben but running his big toe along Felicity's exhausted cunt lips in a way that would have been quite exciting had they been less sore, had she been less tired. As it was, the sensation was just lovely.

"Love you," Felicity sputtered out through sudden, heaving sobs. Aaron climbed up and wrapped her in his whip-tight arms and she sobbed more deeply still. Ben, sleeping, nuzzled her armpit comfortingly. "God! Aaron," Felicity whispered, "how is this going to work?"

"Felicity, lucky lady, we have walked through the Valley of the Shadow of Death together. We came out together. We'll manage together now." Softly, he kissed her brow.

"Much better than you used to be with blubbering women," Felicity cried against his shoulder.

Aaron laughed. "Had more practice, I suppose. Felicity, if I ask you a question, will you tell me the truth?"

"Of course," Felicity said, feeling sleep begin to take her.

"It wasn't really truth serum, was it?"

"No," she snuffled. Mixing barbiturates and alcohol could be lethal. And really, there was no such thing as truth serum. "Rose water. Does it matter?"

"Nope," Aaron said. "Still want to hear about you and Lisa some time."

She smiled, feeling warmer than anyone ever had a right to feel on a raw spring morning. Felix sauntered back in, apparently assured that his rest would be disturbed no further, and curled himself above Felicity's pillow.

And then Aaron pulled the duvet back over them all and they drifted into sleep.

# Epilogue: Verity

## Truth... and Consequences

It was infuriating, it truly was. Since Lisa had confirmed that the baby was definitely a girl, the boys had committed the unpardonable sin not once but three times: they'd awoken a last-trimester Felicity with their bickering.

Infuriating was hardly the word for it.

They had been fighting over the name the last time. Strictly speaking, Aaron hadn't been fighting, he had been sulking. In typical Aaron fashion, he had announced that he thought it would be appropriate that their child be named after his late mother, Eva, and had left it at that — well, that, and broadcasting loud silence whenever another possibility was mentioned. Aaron, the orphan. Their Richie Rich.

It had been Ben who had done most of the bickering, Ben the twin who came from an enormous family. He had insisted that they should name the baby after his mother, who, they were astonished to discover, was actually named Boudicca.

Felicity had been so depressed by the battle that she had been unwilling to enter the fray and suggest her own beloved grandmother's name: Verity. She had merely told them both that they were being childish, morbid... and obscenely inconsiderate, given how hard it was for her to sleep in her distended state.

They'd all agreed, finally, that the last name should be Harris-Marcovitz — Ben and Aaron's last names, hyphenated. As Felicity had patiently explained, no one would ever question who the child's mother was. Given the unconventional domestic arrangement, it seemed sensible to make Ben and Aaron's joint fatherhood very clear. But they'd never settled on a first name, and Felicity despaired of coming to any kind of consensus.

This evening, awakened for the fourth time, Felicity tried hard to get back to sleep, but it was impossible. Aaron was the one doing the insisting, and his voice had a desperate undertone to it that set Felicity's teeth on edge, even as it broke her heart. That, and mild contractions where reminding her of pain soon to come.

"Have a heart, Ben. You're surrounded by people who are yours. You've always had a family. The only relatives I've ever known were some distant cousins and my mom's lawyer, who doesn't exactly count. Can you blame me for hoping she comes out with black hair and brown eyes?"

"Dude," Ben wheedled, "everything you've ever had has been yours. I know it's hard, but your life is full of one-of-kind this and unique that. I've had to share fucking everything — even you with Lici and Lici with you. I just want a child that I know is mine."

"I've always shared you and Felicity," Aaron sighed.

Ben sighed, an octave lower. "Maybe it'll be a red-head — that could be either one of us."

"Nah," Aaron muttered. "Linked gene — remember what Lici said? If my mum had passed red on to me, I'd have come out auburn or dark brown, not black-haired."

"Well," Felicity said, as tartly as she could manage, rolling over and staring down at them, where they were sitting against the bottom posts of the bed, "I'm glad one of you actually listened to something I said, even if it wasn't the bit about not waking me, or the bit about never calling me that fucking name — "

They both gaped at her, clearly deeply sorry that they'd disturbed her sleep. Then they both looked at each other and smiled. "But Lici..."

She growled and tried to sit up — not an easy task when you're carrying an extra forty pounds. "Look, you two, you know I only put up with it from Alexei because he couldn't handle anything more than two syllables at a time. Now if one of my child's fathers isn't able to do better than that — "

They both laughed, and climbed up the bed to either side of her, kissing her as they came.

"That's more like it," she said, trying to sound just as arch, trying not to sound as if she were about to giggle. "In the first place, the two of you know perfectly well we have no way of knowing whose sperm it actually was." That night was a bit of a blur for all three of them. "In the second place, what difference does it really make? And in the third place, I'm tired, you've woken me, and I expect the two of you to make me comfy."

Hands began to grope.

"No, not that way, you adolescent nitwits." Felicity did giggle, finally, even as her annoyance blossomed. "Yes, I know, it's supposed to encourage the softening of the cervix, but I told you, I'm tired, and I have no interest in rewarding the two of you for waking me."

The hands continued to explore, and lips.

"Oh, fine." She pushed down on both of them, lifting herself laboriously up and climbing out of the bed. "I'm going to take a bath. I've got some nasty psychoactives that I will happily use on whichever reprobate..." An implosion of pain sucked her in. It felt as if every muscle in her lower body was attempting to pull itself loose from her skeleton all at once. "Oh, FUCK!" she howled.

When awareness returned, it brought a sweet smell, the sight of both boys gaping at her in concern, the trickle of some fluid down her legs, and the sound of her own disembodied voice saying, "I think it's time to call Lisa, don't you?"

•••

Some fifteen hours later, Felicity was in bed again — a different bed — a baby happily attempting to nurse, Lisa gingerly attempting to heal some of the damage occasioned by the baby's arrival, and a feeling of exhausted fulfillment suffusing her weary, untethered body.

Their faces glowing with awe and a kind of fear she had never seen in them, not even during the years when they were risking their lives on a regular basis just for fun, the boys were whispering again, at the foot of the hospital bed. This time the conversation involved a lot of mutual nodding, and so she happily left them to it.

"How you doing?" asked Lisa as she gently cleaned Felicity off.

"Wonderful," sighed Felicity. "Hurts, but it feels wonderful."

Lisa smiled. "Sort of like losing your virginity, only a thousand times more so."

"Hmmm. That's just about right.... I do feel a kind of like a sail someone's forgotten to pull in...."

Laughing, Lisa finished her exam. "Yeah, that'll get better. I'd better move up there," the doctor said, looking around at her twin brother and Aaron, who were still deep in conversation. "If I keep playing around between your legs, Ben's going to start turning green soon."

"Keep playing around between my legs, and you're going to make Aaron very happy," Felicity joked, surprised she had it in her.

"Well," Lisa said with a smirk, "we can't have that. Especially as poor Connor would be broken-hearted to have missed it."

"Hmmm." Felicity was focused down at the baby. Wheat hair, cornflower eyes. "Connor?"

Lisa prodded at Felicity's exposed breast. "Oh, good, you're expressing collostrum... My lovely husband and our lovely sons are out in the waiting room with the rest of the horde. Mmm. You should be letting down properly in the next few days..."

"Horde?" Felicity asked, fatigue pulling at her.

Lisa's face twisted into a bemused smile as she backed up and removed her no-longer white robes. "These two were taking turns helping you and making calls." She turned to Aaron and Ben. "I can probably hold them off for another twenty minutes. You might want to get to know your new daughter."

The boys looked up at Lisa and — without even getting up — pulled her into a stifling hug.

"Thanks, sis," Ben said.

Lisa turned a deep red, muttered, "You're welcome," and tried to extricate herself.

Once her friend had fought free, Felicity looked down to where her child's fathers were sitting, looks of unaccustomed solemnity on their faces. "Calls?" she asked.

The serious expressions melted to sheepishness — one Felicity was much more familiar with. Ben murmured, "Well, I contacted my family..."

"And I called your folks. And. One or two others. Friends and such," Aaron said.

Lisa laughed. "Both sets of grandparents have been out there for hours. They're positively vibrating. Seamus and Scott are there — watch the stuffed animals, you wouldn't believe what they put in some of the ones they gave Billy. A couple of your lab friends, whose names I can never remember. Uncle Harry's passing around a flask of bourbon. Oh, and just about everyone wanted to know if you needed help with a name."

Ben moaned. Aaron said, "No, we don't need help."

Lisa laughed again, and so did Felicity, shaking the nipple out of the baby's mouth, which set her thinly wailing. "Well," Lisa said, once Felicity had settled her back on the breast, "I'd better go try and keep the natives from becoming too restless. See you lot in a bit," Lisa said as she left the room.

Ben and Aaron seemed to have rematerialized on either side of the bed, looking at the baby so adoringly that what was left of Felicity's middle started to melt.

"She's...." Aaron looked for the word and failed.

"Beautiful," Ben supplied, and it was a judgment they both seemed content with.

Felicity found tears dripping down from her nose onto the fine fair hair. "I was blonde till I was three or so," she said, looking up at them, "and Caucasian babies often start with blue eyes...."

"Doesn't matter," Ben sighed.

"Not at all," Aaron agreed.

Felicity cried some more.

"And about the name," Aaron said. "We were thinking, maybe..."

The two of them looked to each other, then to her. Together they said, "Lici?"

When Felicity's jaw dropped, they both laughed. "Sorry," Aaron said. "Just kidding."

Ben ran his fingers through the baby's hair. "Actually, we wanted to ask you something." He looked up to Aaron.

"We were actually thinking," Aaron said, resting a finger on the infant's cheek, still stained by birth, "of asking you what you might think...." He looked into her eyes, then up at Ben.

"Given how this all started with a game of Truth and Dare... We wondered if you'd thought of naming her after your grandmother."

Felicity looked down at the miniscule miracle that was snoring at her incredibly sore breast. "Verity," she said, tears flowing again.

# Folding Herself In

## Sometimes the surprise comes after the bachelor party

"Can't believe we're actually sitting here quietly like it's just another Friday night," Gil muttered, taking a pull from the bottle of vintage port that Shawn had bought him as a joke. He'd already polished off an impressive amount of the vodka that Frank had provided.

"Well," Shawn said, waving his eighth snifter of whiskey at the disaster that was their apartment, "we had a nice little stag bash, didn't we? Sent your brothers and the guys home properly drunk."

"*Home*, yeah, right," Gil snorted. "Will, maybe. James, sure. But I'd be willing to bet that the twins and Frank, Scotty and them are off giving our single days a proper send off, and here we are winding down for a good night's sleep. I mean…"

Smiling, Shawn said, "I suppose I know what you mean. But I'm not planning on getting a whole hell of a lot of sleep *tomorrow* night. You?"

Gil blushed, as Shawn had known that he would — whether at the idea of Shawn enjoying *conjugal relations* with Gil's sister or at Gil's own soon-to-be-legitimate debauchery with his long-time girlfriend Phoebe, Shawn wasn't sure. "No," he grunted, taking another swig.

They sat there in silence, surveying the thoroughly be-messed living room for some minutes. Shawn knew that they should clean up — this apartment would be Gil and Phoebe's after the honeymoon, and she wasn't likely to appreciate coming home for the first time to upturned furniture and four-letter words painted on the walls. Still they sat, however, more than mildly drunk and hugely content.

He was *marrying Diana*. Unbelievable. It was if his whole life — every horrible accident and wonderful, serendipitous happenstance had been pushing him to this place, this time. Into her thin, strong arms. Her thin, strong fingers…

After tomorrow, no more having to sneak or hide. He could take her hand, tell her and Gil's parents that they were going upstairs, and fuck her until she screamed, and nobody would mind. They'd probably be *pleased!*

"We're marrying them," Gil said blinking up at the letters sprayed on the wall opposite: *Bullshit!* it read in alternating purple and red.

"Yeah," Shawn answered.

"Fuck," Gil said.

"Yeah."

"You… happy?"

"Oh, yes," Shawn said.

Gil grinned. "Me too." He lifted the port, Shawn lifted his whiskey, and for the fiftieth time that night, they toasted their luck.

Putting down the glass, Shawn knocked over one of the bottles of lube that Frank had given them as a joke. After another silence, he asked, "What do you think the girls are up to?"

"Well, I know Connie and F'licia were going to throw them a bachelorette party, but come on," Gil said dismissively, "you know Phoebe's had them both home and in bed for hours."

Shawn nodded and glanced at his watch: almost 1:00. "Speaking of which — "

A loud *thunk* sounded from the front door, and then two more.

"Fuck," Gil grumbled, "that's got to be the twins come back to paint on the walls some more."

Shawn waited for Gil to get the door; his friend barely moved.

Three more *thunks* thudded against the door.

Resenting having to budge from his comfy chair, Shawn groaned his way to his feet and shuffled over to the door. "Fine, fine," he grumbled, reaching out to the nob.

Opening the door, he expected to find Gary and Jerry, drunk out of their skulls. Or perhaps Scotty held up by Tom and Liam.

What he didn't expect to find was Ruth Thorson, one of his and Diana's brainiest and quietest friends, standing at an angle with her lipstick smeared (since when did Ruth wear lipstick?), her blouse unbuttoned to her navel, and her black skirt down around her hips, revealing a red lace bra and sky blue panties.

At least she was wearing a bra and panties. "Hullo, Shawn. I'm very invert... inebriate."

"Uh. Hello, Ruth." Shawn was having a hard time not staring down his friend's unsuspectedly canyonous cleavage. "Uh. How was Phoebe and Diana's bachlorette party?"

"Still going," Ruth sighed. She threw her arms around Shawn's neck and gave his cheek a wet kiss. "Mmmmm. Hullo, Gilbert," she said blearily, stumbling towards Gil, her breasts rubbing past Shawn's chest in a really diverting way.

Gil blinked at Ruth as she floated across the room toward him. "Damn, Ruth. You're plowed."

She stopped and looked down. "No, Gilbert. I don't seem to have any furrows on me." Stepping toward him again, she tripped over an empty bottle and flopped across Gil's knees. "Wee!"

Gil stared down at Ruth's backside — the skirt had now flopped up onto her back, revealing her panties not only to be blue, but semi-transparent. His chin trembling uncertainly, his hands gripping the arms of the chair, Gil looked to Shawn for aid.

Transfixed by a backside as surprisingly round as the topside had proved to be, Shawn was at a loss to give any. "Uh... Ruth?"

"Wee!" their friend giggled again, wriggling face-down across

Gil's lap. Gil remained motionless.

"Ruth," Shawn repeated somewhat more steadily, "what brings you here?"

"Well," Ruth said, still folded across Gil's thighs, "Diana and Phoebe wouldn't let me share, so I decided I'd come here and be your Jonny."

Over the years, Shawn had learned to count to ten to give himself time to think Ruth's statements through. Knowing himself to be somewhat plowed, he counted a full fifteen. "I'm sorry, Ruth," he said finally, "I don't understand."

Gil nodded enthusiastically, his eyes fixed on the ceiling — as far from Ruth's backside as he could get them.

"Oh," Ruth said in tone of the mildest possible surprise. She began to push herself upright, one hand on the floor, the other on… some part of Gil that caused his eyes to bulge. She wobbled to a standing position, teetered and plopped back into Gil's lap, sitting this time. "I fell," she said, her head lolling back against Gil's shoulder.

Gil squeaked. Shawn hadn't heard him squeak in years.

"Ruth," Shawn said, trying to keep his I-may-be-drunk-but-I'm-reasonable voice going, "I'm afraid we're still in the dark as to why you're here."

"Ah," Ruth said. "Well, I told you. I tried to climb up on the table with Phoebe and Diana and Jonny, but they wouldn't share."

"On the table?" Gil rumbled.

"Yes. I said. Phoebe and Diana and Jonny where there on the table. I would have folded myself in anywhere, you know."

"What were they doing on the table?" Gil asked.

Shawn had a very vivid idea of where this was headed, but somehow couldn't manage to stop the train.

"Well, Gilbert, I would have thought that was obvious. I've heard you and Phoebe often enough that I know you've got a clairly fear idea…" Ruth shook her head, her hair flying in Gil's face, and she giggled. "Fair. Ly. Clear."

Shawn's stomach seemed to be filling with something cold

and heavy.

"Gilbert, I wish you wouldn't keep poking my butt, it's distracting," said Ruth, wriggling in a very distracting manner.

"So," Shawn managed to say, praying against all odds that this would all end well, "Jonny… took his clothes off?" Jonny had been part of their group of friends after college — well, part of the *girls'* circle, anyway. Shawn'd always found him incredibly self-involved. And *pretty*.

Ruth nodded and began to sway against Gil, causing him to begin to turn even a deeper shade of red. She began to sing breathily, "'I want to be, a…' Did you know he's been working as an escort? Really a good job for him, I think, suits his temperament and his skill set quite nicely. In any case, I always find having sex with him nice — his stamina is rather remarkable — and of course, I've always wanted to have sex with Diana, and Phoebe too, when it comes to that — "

"Sex," Gil said. Well, it was more a hiss than a statement, really. "Sex. Phoebe. Jonny. Sex."

"Oh, yes," Ruth said. "He'd already done quite a nice job with Diana, you see — and Diana really had done a nice job of entertaining Phoebe in the meantime, she really does have the most talented tongue, that girl."

Shawn groaned.

"In any case, when he began to take care of Phoebe — " Gil echoed Shawn's groan. " — Diana looked so all alone, and so nice, and I thought I'd go on up with them and help out, but — "

"They said no," Shawn muttered.

"Yes," pouted Ruth, "they wouldn't share, and Felicia and Connie started pulling me down, and I never did like them, you know, though Susan and Tila were trying to talk them into at least letting me watch from up close, which I thought was rather nice. But Fellatia and Connili… Connie pulled me down, and Diana said she wanted them to herself — "

"Wanted…?" Shawn began, knowing he didn't really want to finish the question, absolutely certain he didn't want an answer.

"Phoebe and Jonny, of course. And I thought…" She peered around the room. "Did you not have stripers? Connie and Felicia swore that you were having stripers — which they very clearly understood to mean *having* stripers, which I have to imagine means something thoroughly sexual — swore that Liam and Tom swore that Frank swore that you'd have them, and that was the only reason that they were able to talk Phoebe or Diana into it. What's good for the gander is really good for the goose, you know."

"Not *stripers*, Ruth. *Strippers*." Trying not to watch Gil's face growing dangerously red, trying not to stare at the way the blonde hair was peeking around the crotch of Ruth's panties beneath the useless skirt, Shawn said, "Ruth. Ruth. Our strippers were Gary and Jerry in drag. It was one of the most disgusting things I've ever seen."

"Sex. Phoebe," Gil moaned. His eyes snapped to Ruth's; she returned his stare with an equanimity that was all the greater for being utterly trashed. "*Sex*. Phoebe would *never*… No fucking way! With Jonny fucking Powers?"

*With Diana*, Shawn thought, and in spite of himself, he felt his libido stir to life, jealousy and horniness its favorite meals.

Ruth blinked at Gil and then pointed at where *Bullshit!* was painted over the fish tank. "Your wall doesn't agree with you, Gilbert." She finished this pronouncement very seriously, but then giggled. "I do think she liked the bit with Diana best."

Both men stood, Gil toppling Ruth to the ground.

"Wee!" she giggled. "Was sex with the twins fun?"

"I'll *kill* him!" Gil bellowed.

Shawn nodded, but a part of him wanted to watch for a bit, and *then* kill them.

"Can't get in, you know," Ruth said. "Private. Invitation only. And you know, Gilbert, Phoebe will only think that you didn't want her to have what you got. She won't like that. *Patriarchal, sexist attitude*." This last was declaimed in so Phoebe-like a tone that it brought both Gil and Shawn up short. "And you know what Diana's like when she's disappointed, Shawn. She'll be *sooo* disappointed, I think, if you interrupt. Well, I suppose you didn't *both* have sex with your stripers, did — "

"*We didn't have sex with my... STRIPPERS, Ruth!*" Gil yelled, still glaring toward the door.

She winked. Ruth Thorson, of all people, *winked.* "Oh, of course. What a shame. Gary and Jerry. I've always rather wanted that experience, myself." Ruth smiled blissfully at Gil and then at Shawn. "Well, how nice! I'm glad that I've come after all. I *can* be your Jonny."

Shawn felt Gil turn with him to look at Ruth again. She was sprawled against the chair where Gil had dumped her, legs spread, hair wild.

She was unbuttoning what little was left to unbutton of her blouse. "'Macho, macho man,'" she sang breathily, baring one shoulder and then the other.

"Ruth," Shawn said, knowing that he had very little leeway here — if he didn't do something soon, either Jonny Powers was going to have to eat through a straw and pee through a tube or Ruth was going to have more drunken revenge sex coming at her than she could possibly know —

"I rather like having sex with men whose adrenaline is running high," Ruth sighed, removing her blouse and tossing it in Gil's face. "It's so exciting. Sex with angry women isn't anywhere nearly as much fun."

The bra was semi-transparent too, it seemed, and Shawn was fascinated to discover that Ruth's left nipple was pierced.

Dropping to his knees between Ruth's thighs, Gil worked at the blouse that he had balled in his hands. "Is he? Really? Fucking?"

"Oh, yes," Ruth said, wriggling the skirt past her feet, "and Phoebe was making that high-pitched sighing *OH-OH-OH* sound she always makes when Diana and I come to visit and you and she are off — *OH!*" *Away* went the blouse, *rip* went the brassiere and *slurp* went Gil's mouth as he pulled the ringed nipple into his mouth. Shawn watched in a kind of fascinated dread as Gil's hands made Ruth's panties disappear as effectively as they'd eliminated the bra, and suddenly there was no pretense — Ruth Thorson was quite naked on the floor of their apartment, and Gil was moving his thumb up and down her vulva in a manner that caused Ruth's wide-set eyes to cross. "How nice," she said.

Shawn stood there, frozen. Really, he had never been one to lock up. When decisive action was called for, Shawn was always the first to commit — a tendency that Gil and Phoebe had been trying to rein in for a decade.

Not Diana. She'd never tried to make him be someone else.

But here he was, watching as one of his best friends diddled one of his fiancée's best friends, watching Ruth attempting to undo the zipper to Gil's trousers by main force, and Shawn couldn't move, couldn't think, couldn't speak. Stop them? Join them? Go to bed? Go to Connie and Felicia's and bay at the windows like a lovesick hound smelling a bitch in heat? Two. *Two.*

Three.

"You know, Shawn," Ruth said over Gil's shoulder — she had apparently opened his fly and was worming her hand in; Gil had switched to the unadorned breast — "Do you know — OH! Goodness, Gilbert, what nice hands you have! — I've wanted to fuck you both since we met at that birthday part of Diana's, and the thoughts were so clear and I — *MMMM* — kept laughing, the thought of you both wrapped around me like bread on a sandwich..." Ruth's hands were working manically at Gil's shirt, but her voice was as calm as always — with occasional outbursts of sexual transport. "And Diana does say that your mouth is so nice, Shawn, I bet it's as good as *hers!*"

Gil plunged a finger into Ruth, causing her back to arch. His long thumb kept up its wild dance at the front of her pussy — which was reddening and slickening as Shawn watched.

Shawn's cock was as hard as he could ever remember it being. Diana had never made him this hard.

He had never forced himself to wait this long with Diana.

*Jonny's dark flesh, stallion-long, plunging into pale and pink and copper...* He shook his head.

"Oh!" Ruth said, voice still airy and distracted — and Shawn could see a reason for the distraction for a change, as he watched Gil add a second finger. "Do. Come fuck. Shawn. *Please.*" She pushed herself up into the chair, yanking Gil by his shirt so that he stood beside her, his crotch at her face level. Shawn watched in awe as she drew Gil's enormous erection out of his trousers.

*Damn! Not a stallion, but...*

Ruth lowered her mouth to that amazing piece of befreckled manhood. Gil threw back his head and groaned, his hands flying to her hair.

Ruth began humming "Macho Man" as she slurped him into her mouth. One hand stroked Gil's cock in time with her lips while the other slipped between her round thighs and began to stroke at her pussy.

Shawn had walked in on Gil and Phoebe once — they apparently hadn't had the restraint to make it all of the way back to Gil's room — but all that Shawn had gotten was an eyeful of bountiful, bouncing breasts, since though her blouse had been quite gone they hadn't removed her skirt. He had only seen one cunt in his life, and it was thin-lipped and topped with a tuft of obsidian-black hair.

Ruth's was amazing, but very, very different. Exotic and puffy, it seemed to be calling him from across the room while Ruth's pale eyes seemed to plead with him vaguely from the other end of her as her cheeks filled and hollowed.

Gil turned his head toward Shawn; his jaw was slack and his eyes wide. "Damn, Shawn. Come on."

"I... I don't know if I can," Shawn groaned.

"Shawn — *Nnnnnn* — my fucking sister spread her legs — "

Ruth spoke around Gil's penis. "Actually, she was on all fours. *Phoebe* spread — "

With a growl, Gil thrust into her mouth.

Shawn's feet led him to the chair. His knees gave way, placing him level with Ruth. She smiled and sucked. Gil was beginning to pant.

Shawn reached out and ran his thumb up the length of Ruth's lips as Gil had done; she shivered, causing the ring to bounce against her round left breast. Decisiveness flooded back into Shawn sure and simple, and with the same certainty with which he had gone off to slay monsters and rescue fair maidens (and others), he bent forward and kissed the nearly hidden bud of Ruth's clit.

They say that smell is the most primal of the senses, connected to the most primitive part of the brain, and so tied closely to memories. Taste is a close second though, and the minute Shawn's tongue began to lap at Ruth, her tang sent him back into his mind to another night just before a wedding, Will and Nancy's, when he'd been slightly less drunk but a lot more anxious. Diana had talked Gil into switching rooms without telling Shawn. He had been about to pull his I'm-not-good-enough-for-you, I'm-going-to-be-gone-at-the-end-of-the-summer act again, terrified as he was that he wouldn't be able to let her go if she so much as touched him. She hadn't touched him, not at first. She had simply removed her clothing. Very slowly. Silently. Her eyes still on his, challenging, pleading, she had climbed into the bed next to him, and waited. She hadn't had to wait long.

They hadn't fucked that first night — neither of them felt ready, or at least *Shawn* hadn't, and Diana had respected that. But they did explore in other ways, and after she had timidly kissed him to an explosive ejaculation — white droplets like pearls in her hair — he had returned the favor, kissing at her privates and then lapping at them, catlike.

The look of astonishment on Diana's face when she had come had filled Shawn with more pride and joy than any other single accomplishment that he could remember.

Ruth's tasted similar, tangy and tart, but the texture against his tongue, around his fingers was quite different. And the sounds…

Ruth loosed a muffled shriek, her cunt pulsing against Shawn's mouth, and Gil howled. Shawn knew that howl well, though he'd never been in the same room before when it was bellowed. Shawn's friend collapsed to the floor, his cock splattering come across Ruth's body and Shawn's face. "Damn," Gil said, and blinked. "Sorry. Damn."

"'S all right," Shawn muttered, wiping his cheek with his sleeve. "Well, that was nice…"

"Oh, no, Shawn," Ruth burbled, her eyes bright as Shawn had never seen them. "It wouldn't do for you to leave now. I really do want to make you come, you know."

"Uh…"

"Also," she continued, her tone returning to its normal airiness, "I still want someone inside of me."

"No problem," grunted Gil. He stood, and Shawn was astonished to note that Gil was still hard. He lifted Ruth into the air — "Wee!" — sat in her place, and lowered her back onto his lap.

"Oh, how nice," purred Ruth, arranging her knees on either side of his hips and lowered herself onto his stiff, speckled cock. "*OH*, yes, *very* nice!"

Shawn began to back away, but Ruth arched around toward him. "Well, Shawn, what would you like? You can fuck my bottom, or Gilbert and I can take turns licking you."

Gil blinked.

"Uh, not that, Ruth, no," sputtered Shawn.

"Oh, good," Ruth said. "I've always enjoyed anal sex, especially when I've got something occupying my vagina. I've never had penises in both at the same time, however."

Again Shawn's body began moving before his mind had really absorbed the situation, let alone considered the proposition. He had dropped his pants and shuffled back to where Ruth's plump, moonlike bottom was rising and setting on Gil's horizon before he had time to think.

She had a tattoo in the shape of an arrow point down the small of her back that was made up of the words *Yes she said yes I will yes.*

"Here," Ruth said, leaning over and grabbing the bottle of lube and opening it expertly with one hand while she continued to ride Gil. Reaching out, she smoothed the slick liquid over Shawn's cock, leaving him breathless. "Oh, what a nice penis you have, Shawn. It's just perfect. *Ahhh!*" Ruth gasped as Gil began nibbling on her nipples.

Touching his cock, Shawn realized that it was as slick as ice in a warm drink. Lovely or not, its need was urgent. Shawn's hunger howled as he reached trembling hands out and touched Ruth's soft, white haunch, stopping her in mid-bounce.

"Oh, just wait a nanosecond," she managed to murmur — Gil was continuing his assault on her breasts — as she squeezed what seemed like most of what remained of the lube onto two of her fingers and deftly worked it up her ass. Then her fingers slid out and it was there, waiting for him. Open. Glistening.

Grasping his erection by the base in numb fingers, Shawn whimpered as his cock touched Ruth's puckered rear hole, pressed, and pushed through the tight ring of muscle.

"*FUCK!*" all three of them cried out.

Shawn was only a few inches in — two thirds of his cock still waited outside of her ass — but as he began to thrust in as gently as he could manage, he could feel Gil's cock jumping inside of her cunt through the thin membrane separating the two passages. Shawn felt Gil's huge hands clamp over his own; together they kept Ruth still as they began to move together inside of her.

"*FUCK!*" the usually demure Ruth screamed as they began to find a rhythm together, thrusting up into her, front and back. "*FUCKING FUCK! DAMN!*" Her head was flung back against Shawn's shoulder, her chest against Gil's face. She was flush from her nipples up, and a string of most un-Ruth-like obscenity spewed from her mouth. "*GOD! FUCK MY...! FUCK!*"

Her bottom was tight; even with the lube it took him two minutes of thrusting before he felt his balls brush against Gil's and he knew that he was all of the way in.

He and Diana had tried anal sex twice — once by accident when they'd been fucking for so long that Shawn had flipped her, pushed in, and only realized that he'd pressed into the wrong entry when she squawked. In her shock she had squeezed him so hard that, even after three rounds earlier that day, he had came instantly. They'd tried it again on his most recent birthday, but while he had loved it, she had complained of discomfort afterward, and so Shawn hadn't suggested it again. There were plenty of other ways to play, and he didn't want his playmate

Ruth seemed to be enjoying herself enormously.

Shawn was going to have to ask Frank about that lubrication.

That was if he ever had a reason to sleep with Diana again.

The wedding.

Could they get married now?

Shawn loved Gil. He loved Ruth, after a fashion — at the moment, his hips slapping against her bottom as Gil's thighs squeezed Shawn's, he loved her a *lot* — but even buried in another woman's ass and with full certainty that Diana'd had Jonny Powers buried in *her*, Shawn was certain as he could have been that Diana was the person he wanted to wake up to for the rest of his life, that he wanted to have children with, that he could see himself growing old beside, that he could trust to stand beside him in sickness and in health.

*Trust.*

He and Diana were going to have a *very* interesting conversation tomorrow. Later today. Before the wedding if he could manage it. After if need be.

"*GuguEWR-AAAAAAAAAAAAAA!*" Ruth screamed as Shawn and Gil slammed into her from either side. She pulled Shawn's hands from her hips up to her breasts, where Gil was still grazing. Gil's cock thrusting along the length of Shawn's own. The tight loop of Ruth's ass squeezing him tight, *pulsing.*

A scream answered by two more as first Shawn and then Gil poured into Ruth's body.

Breathless, slick, they collapsed.

"Fuck," Gil gasped.

Shawn's softening cock twitched, triggering another spasm through Ruth, followed by a giggle. "Bread around a sandwich," she sighed followed by a last, diffuse, "Wee!"

Shawn could feel Gil's breath hot on his neck as they both laughed limply.

"I hope I can walk for the wedding," Ruth said. "I wouldn't want to miss that."

Shawn saw Gil's brow furl, guilt and uncertainty playing across his friend's broad, open face. Gil and Phoebe had never seemed to trust each other or themselves quite as much as Shawn and Diana did. "'S all right, Gil," Shawn said. He kissed the back of Ruth's neck.

"Hmmm," she murmured. "'I want to be... a macho man...'"

And with that, she passed out.

Shawn backed away from Ruth, his softening cock disengaging from her ass with a loud *plop*. She shuddered and curled tighter around Gil.

Gil, who was panting. Staring wide-eyed at Shawn. "Damn. Shawn. We just... Phoebe'll *kill* me."

"You can take turns killing each other," Shawn said, trying to calm the tumult in his own chest.

"I... How can we get...?"

"Talk to her, Gil. They're going to feel just as terrible as we do."

"But we aren't supposed to... Before the..."

"Talk to her."

Gil nodded, "Yeah. *Talk*." He looked up at Shawn over Ruth's slumped head, his face contorted as if he were working on a particularly challenging engineering problem. "I just... I couldn't stand it if... She doesn't handle booze well, Phoebe. I know she only did it 'cause she was drunk and 'cause she thought I..." Gil blinked and stroked Ruth's back, then gave a small grin and looked back up at Shawn. "I... I've always wanted to..."

In spite of the nagging sobriety that was creeping over him,

Shawn smiled. Ruth's face was slack on Gil's shoulder; naked on his friend as she was, Shawn found to his surprise that she was quite beautiful. "Yeah," he said. "That was pretty amazing. I've always wondered what it would be like with her."

"Oh. Yeah. That too," Gil said, and then, for some reason, blushed. "Think we should try to get her home?"

"Let's put her in my bed. I'll sleep out here." Shawn murmured, his eyes still moving over Ruth's form. "If the girls come over... Well, I wake faster than you do."

"True," Gil said with a weak grin. He stood, still holding Ruth.

Her legs wrapped instinctively around his waist. "'I want to live at the Y... M... mmm... C...'" She buried her face in Gil's neck and fell back to snoring.

"Need a hand?"

"No," Gil sighed, shifting his hands to her ass. "Shawn... Do you...? Are we going to be okay?"

"Yeah, Gil," Shawn sighed, righting the sofa and pulling a blanket from one of the ferns. "We'll be just fine."

# Over the Top

## A Friend (or Two) in Need Is a Friend (or Two) Indeed

The scratching sound from the ceiling begins again, and Danny groans. Within a minute, a soft, rhythmic thumping joins in time with the scraping, and he curls in upon himself, trying to bury his head under the pillow.

He could have chosen the cabin's upstairs bedroom — the one that is usually Danny's mom and dad's — but he thought it was polite to let Luz and Jamie have it. It is bigger, after all.

A soft sigh from above penetrates his pillow, and he finds himself answering it with a whimper.

They've been planning on coming up here after graduation, just the four of them, for a year. It's been a kind of schoolboy fantasy of being grownups, running off to the woods for a couple of weeks, away from the world, away from parents.... No one to watch who slept in which bedroom.

Finally. Fucking. Finally, finally fucking. Fantasy, sure, but unspoken promise as well. Sex in the cabin. Sex by the lake. Two couples, each doing what couples do.

Only that was before Suzie and Danny decided to be mature and break it off, since they were going to different colleges and long-distance relationships never work. Danny was the idiot to start that conversation. Suzie somberly told him two days before they left that she'd taken a job waiting tables with her friend Alice, the ditz, so she wouldn't be coming and making things uncomfortable. So: one couple. And Danny. No more schoolboy fantasy. Not for him, anyway.

Besides, even an idiot like Danny can see that Luz clearly isn't a schoolboy. Strictly speaking, neither are Jamie and Danny any more. And Jamie and Luz have been acting very much their age.

A giggle upstairs breaks the steady rhythm of scrape-sigh-thud, scrape-sigh-thud.

Blessedly, Danny has only actually walked in on them once, the second day after they came up to the woods. Danny was just coming back from a run around the lake, and his friends had apparently surprised themselves by succumbing to their own desires in the living room. The image of Luz's breasts gamboling against the cushion of the old couch that Jamie was leaning her over took an immediate and indelible place in Danny's imagination.

For two days after that, the three of them went about their business in utter silence. Cooking. Reading. Danny went fishing a lot. Not a word. Ms. Prince, the school librarian, would have been proud.

He's been very careful to let them know that he's going out for a walk every evening at sundown. That he won't be back for an hour or two. So they don't worry about him getting lost or anything.

And so since that one day, they've mostly restricted their more amorous activities to when he's out of the cabin. It hasn't stopped them from kissing and touching and sighing and making Danny want to hit them both.

And of course, every night, after they think he's asleep, Jamie and Luz engage in a particularly energetic, particularly bed-moving, particularly wall-banging fuck. Or two. Ten feet over his head.

In his mind's eye, Danny sees her now, right above him, on her hands and knees. Her bathrobe — was he too stupid to see her nipples through the fabric before, or is he just imagining them when he sees her now? — is piled up over her ass: round, and magnificent, jiggling with Jamie's thrusts, jiggling in time with her swaying breasts.

Jamie groans.

Maybe she is on her back, her thighs flushing dark on the insides where Jamie's hips slap against them, Jamie, his mouth open and eyes shut, Luz, her head thrown back...

Suzie, the soft, pale flesh of her belly beneath his lips, scent of flowers, a hungry whimper as he presses himself between her legs...

For the third time that day, Danny feels himself stiffening, his cock swelling within the hand that has unconsciously looped itself around the one piece of his flesh that no one else has ever poked at — flesh private to himself.

And, on thirteen miraculous occasions over the past year, Suzie. Her clever fingers slipping past the waistband of his jeans and evoking sensations that Danny would never have believed possible. All that sniggering about whacking off from the other guys, Jamie's sighing Luz's name in the bathroom, and Danny never knew. Never understood how flesh on flesh can perform such magic, can coax you out of yourself.

Now he knows. Now he can't stop. How can he have waited so long? And why can't he help himself now? What the hell is wrong with him?

The first time that Suzie rubbed him to explosion, after they'd been going out most of junior year, he cried after he came and she cradled him, kissing his forehead. And then he slipped his fingers beneath her skirt, past the elastic of her panties' leg to the moist, warm flesh beneath, and, trembling in the back seat of her parents' car, she showed him how to return the favor.

And he always stopped them from from going too quickly. From going too far.

Fuck.

That is where he longs to be now. Going too far. Cuddled against her secret flesh, his own cock pressing into her…

Luz screams Jamie's name, and the bed above slams against the wall one last time and skids to a stop.

Danny's fingers are stroking, grasping tightly at his cock — the head is dark red and the flesh stings with use and need. He looks down and growls in disgust at himself. I have to take a shower, he thinks, and with great, unwilling determination detaches hand from rod. A girl's high voice sighs Oh, oh, oh, and he can't tell if he's hearing Luz from the room above or Suzie in his own mind, and he knows that if he doesn't do something right now he will go crazy. Crazier. Over the top. And that whacking off isn't doing something. Not any more.

He stumbles into the bathroom and sheds his glasses and pajamas, jumping beneath the shower before he has time to think about the fact that it's going to be frigid; it's been a chilly summer up here in the mountains. The cold water sears his flesh and deflates his erection, and the pain of its shrinking is almost a relief.

Danny's parents talk about love way too much. Their doormat read All You Need Is Love. Love is happiness and Love is the greatest power in the universe on the fridge. Blah, blah, blah. Love.

Danny spent so many of his school year alone. Embraced the fact that no one gave a shit about him except to make fun of the nerd in the Harry Potter glasses. Love wasn't something he wanted to think about. But now… Now he can feel love — his love for Suzie, even though he broke it off with her. Hell, his love for Jamie and Luz — he can feel all of that love twisting him, warping him like the wet clay that Mr. Benson showed them how to shape on a wheel.

Clay: the cool, smooth feel of the wet earth beneath his fingers felt good, and shapes formed — magically formed — as the clay spun between his hands: a lovely flower-blossom cup.

That blew up in the kiln. But Danny didn't care. Much. He made something. And the feel of it, alive and slippery...

Suzie's slit, slick and soft and warm beneath his fingers. Her fingers, slim and strong around his shaft...

Luz's breasts, shock waves rippling through them as Jamie thrusts into her, their love and lust animal and terrible, their faces twisted...

"FUCK!" With a frustrated scream, Danny turns off the water and collapses in the fiberglass tub with a bang. His cock is as erect and demanding now as it ever was, and Danny knows it won't go away, but knows too that if he tries to take care of it now while it is wet or uses soap it will only shred his overused skin until he bleeds and that still won't satisfy its hunger. His hunger. His desire. He kicks the wall of the bath, and then kicks it again. And again. "SHIT!"

The door bursts open and a wide-eyed, wild-haired Luz flies in, Jamie just behind her. Her gown is at best haphazardly closed and even as Danny scrambles to hide himself, to cover his adamant shame, he cannot help but notice a berry-colored blur of a nipple bouncing near the hem.

"Danny!" Luz gasps.

"You... You okay, bro?" asks Jamie, and the only mercy is that there isn't even the hint of a smirk in his friend's voice. "Sounded like you fell!"

"I'm f-f-fine," Danny manages to splutter, but he knows he isn't fooling them, lying there with tears flowing down his wet cheeks and his hands cupped over his engorged penis.

"Oh, Danny," Luz sighs, and her compassion only makes Danny feel worse — or perhaps she is merely giving him permission — and the floodgates open and Danny begins to weep in earnest.

Two sets of hands pull him up, lead him out of the tub, wrap him in a towel and dry him off. Two sets of arms pull him into a warm, trembling hug.

Love.

Through the towel, Danny's cock strains against Luz's round, wide belly.

"Danny," Jamie says, and Danny can hear the hesitancy in his friend's voice. "Danny, how can we...?"

"We're so sorry, Danny. We didn't think of... Of how loud we were being. Right above you. That really wasn't fair of us."

"No, no, no, it's not you," Danny hisses. "It's me. I'm just... twisted. I'm sick. I..."

"You miss her, don't you, Danny," says Jamie, and Danny feels what little blood isn't pooled in his pelvis rushing to his face.

They know. They know how he's aching for Suzie. How he's regretting...

Rubbing himself bloody thinking about...

"Danny, we understand." It is Luz's voice this time and new shame floods Danny, knowing that Luz knows. That Luz, who thinks of him as a friend, as a good guy, knowing that she knows that he dreams of girls' pussies and asses and breasts. Of Luz's pussy even when he dreams of Suzie. "We're sorry, Danny."

"Maybe..." Jamie mutters. "Maybe we can help you out a bit. Maybe Luz..."

"Jamie?" snaps Luz, and Danny feels his innards tear.

"I know what it's like," Jamie snaps back with deadly urgency. "Being around you for months. Wanting to touch you, to... to fuck you and not being able to and feeling like I was going to bloody explode. Like if someone didn't touch me, I was going to fucking die. For real, die."

Danny moans, and he feels Luz shift against him and hates himself for noticing that her cotton-covered nipples are stiffening against his chest and shoulder. Hates himself for noticing that the two of them reek of sex.

"Jamie, are you suggesting...?" Luz begins, but a wet sound

closes her mouth; Jamie has kissed his talk-first girlfriend into silence. The nipples press harder against Danny's flesh, and it is only because he is terrified and because the two of them are already holding him that he restrains his hands from grasping those breasts, from feasting on those nipples, from pulling her... "Danny," Luz says quite breathily. "Danny, I... I could... um, help you. If you wanted. If that didn't seem too disgusting."

"Disgusting?" Danny finally manages to say, an angry laugh. "Why the fucking hell would the idea of you touching me be disgusting?"

"Well," Luz murmurs, "I know I'm not exactly as pretty as Suzie..."

Jamie begins to grumble but Danny once again beats him to it. "Hell of a fucking lot you know. You're fucking gorgeous, Luz. Jamie's the luckiest fucking bastard in the world, and he knows it." Danny can feel her shiver against him, and it doesn't help matters. "But... You two love each other. And I... I love Suzie, and I fucking sent her away like a fucking idiot and I fucking miss her so fucking much and I'm so fucking horny I can't take it, and you two, I don't want you not to enjoy... But the sound or even the thought of the sound fills my fucking head and my fucking body and it makes me so bloody hard, and I... FUCK!" Danny collapses in frustration against his friends' embrace, furious with his body that it doesn't seem to care that Luz is Jamie's girlfriend, not his, that Suzie is the one he wants. Furious with his body that what it really wants to do just now is push his friend up against the counter and shove itself into whatever hole is available.

"Danny," Luz says, and it is the rational, logical Luz voice, the AP Calc voice, and Danny thanks whatever stars are watching over him, because that voice returns him to something like himself. "I'd be happy to help you — but only if you think that it would help. That it wouldn't just make you feel worse."

Too desperate to be shocked, Danny moans, "Please."

Jamie grunts and Luz gives a quick gasp. "Really?"

"Please."

"All right, Danny. All right. I'd be... Um. Wow." Leaning forward, she gives him a quick, fluttery kiss on the lips, and he can feel her grinning against his mouth. Then, stepping back out of the group embrace, she squares her shoulders. "Jamie, Danny, I'll only do this if I know you both understand that it doesn't change anything. That we're still... friends."

"Yeah," said Jamie, and his voice is low with something Danny would guess in a different situation was anger.

Not wanting to think too hard about it, Danny nods emphatically.

Luz speaks again, and her voice is edging higher; she clearly knows they are talking about doing something terribly dangerous. Something potentially really stupid. "Good. And I won't... won't fuck you, Danny, because I know Suzie would never forgive me, and I wouldn't forgive myself. And I won't do anything unless Jamie stays. I don't want you imagining things that didn't happen, love. And I don't want you feeling like we're doing anything sneaky, Danny. Because I..." Something chokes her voice off, and Danny wishes that he could see the blob that is her face more clearly. "Do you both understand?"

In his peripheral vision, Danny sees Jamie's fuzzy profile nodding vigorously. He follows suit.

Trembling hands — Luz's, smooth and fine — take his shoulders and move him back. "Maybe... Here, Danny, why don't you have a seat?"

Suddenly, he is feeling cold — colder than he did in the shower. Shaking, he complies. The wooden lid of the toilet presses up flat against his balls, pushes his erection up into the towel.

Luz is moving in front of him, arranging the bathmat, kneeling down.

"Wait... Uh..." Danny says with a swallow. "Could I...? I'd like to, um, see. May I have my glasses?" Out of the indistinct fog, Danny sees a large hand clutching the familiar black frames. Jamie's hand. "Thanks, bro."

"'Snothing, bro."

Sliding on his glasses, Danny sees them both: Luz, her dark skin pale, eyes wide and bright; Jamie dark with some emotion that Danny can't even begin to fathom. "Guys... You don't have to do this, Luz. I don't... Jamie, it's okay. I'll survive."

A grin flashes across his friend's wide face and he says, "I... I don't mind at all, Dan. As long as it's okay with Luz." He strokes her hair, and she gives a small smile. "It's actually kind of... a turn-on, you know?"

Now Luz's face darkens.

Danny doesn't know, but he doesn't want to ask, doesn't think he can take talking about this much longer.

"Do you know what fellatio is, Danny?" When he shakes his head, Luz continues tentatively. "A, um, blow job?"

"Oh. Uh. Yeah."

She runs her fingers along his towel-covered leg. "Would you like me to do that for you?"

Choking on his heart, Danny glances up at Jamie.

Jamie is grinning even more broadly. "Trust me, Danny, you would like it. Her mouth is amazing."

Gulping for air, Danny gasps, "Okay."

Luz's brown eyes search up into his, and Danny is struck for the first time at just how different this brown is from the bright cinnamon in Suzie's irises. Luz's eyes are dark, piercing... and uncertain, just now.

"Luz," Danny pleads.

She favors him with a nearly imperceptible grin and peels back the towel.

There's a sharp intake of breath, and Danny has no idea which of the three of them took it.

Her fingers, ink-stained, brown, and long, reach out and touch his cock gently.

Another gasp, and this time Danny knows it's his.

"Does mine look that fucking huge?" Jamie groans, his face dark again.

"I'm not going to play adolescent male comparison games,

Jamie. But yes, yours is quite nice."

Her fingers curl around the cock they're both staring at and suddenly Danny can't look anymore. "Oh, god, Luz!"

It's easy to forget, rubbing your prick night after night, day after day, hour after hour, that having someone else rub it is a very different, very nice feeling.

And then Luz — prim, perfect, polite Luz — lowers her mouth to the head of his cock. Circles the head with her tongue. Her eyes on his the entire time.

This is not a nice feeling. It is a feeling that is so good that it hurts.

"Oh, god," Jamie groans.

Suzie offered to do this once, at the end of yet another long make-out session (this one in the back seat of his parents' car), but Danny was so nervous and so eager that he'd spurted before she'd even gotten his fly all of the way down. Suzie didn't mind. At least she said she didn't.

Her lips over her teeth, Luz slowly takes Danny's head into her mouth; he can feel the flare of his helmet pressing against the roof of her mouth. Can feel the bursts of excited breath from her nostrils along his length.

Suzie's mouth, small and hot, her tongue against his, sharp-tipped and searching...

*DNA has four base nucleotides. RNA does as well, but the complimentary base to adenine is uracil instead of...*

"Oh, GOD!" Danny finds his hands fisting in Luz's bushy hair and it is only through a supreme effort of will that he keeps himself from pulling his friend's mouth all the way down the length of his cock. "Fuck, Luz!"

She pulls back off of him just a touch and beams when he whimpers. "Do you like that, Danny?"

"Oh, god! Fuck yesss!"

She takes him back into her mouth, deeper this time, and slowly begins to bob, her fist running up and down his shaft as her tongue swirls over his tip. Glorious.

One night, late, studying at Suzie's for the English final, Mr. Logan's which was notoriously impossible, and after Alice, Luz, and Jamie took off, and Suzie's little sister finally disappeared upstairs, Suzie pounced on him, straddling him in the couch, her hair blinding him, her crotch, thin cotton clad, grinding against his own until she shrieked and he screamed...

"Fuck, Luz, that's so fucking hot," Jamie cries out, and he moves up behind her, his hands running under the gown, a breast bouncing free. A hand running down past her belly, past where Danny can see.

Luz groans around Danny's cock.

"Suck his cock, babe," Jamie growls into her ear. "Take Danny's hard cock in that dirty, smart-ass, bookworm mouth and make him come."

Her eyes still locked on his, Luz's cheeks glow bronze as they fill and hollow. Shame? Desire? With the hand that had been resting on Danny's thigh, she reaches up and roughly squeezes his nipple.

A tingling, like the most painful pins-and-needles ever, a contraction deep within. Suzie, her eyes closed, her cheeks flushed bright red, nipples hard as diamonds as they pound their pelvises together, I'm yours, I'm yours!

"Suzie!"

Even after two rounds of masturbation earlier in the day, the force of the orgasm threatens to destroy Danny. His hips buck and a flood of warmth explodes out of him and into Luz's hot, soft mouth. Not just one pulse but a dozen, each releasing its own bit of the shadow that has been smothering him.

A brief cough, and Luz swallows, releasing his penis from that incredible mouth, staring up into Danny's eyes with a look of ferocious pride.

Then Jamie turns her to him and they kiss, and Danny can see her jaw working as she presses her tongue into Jamie's mouth. Danny's jism into Jamie's mouth.

And Danny can see their bodies arching together, kneeling

there on the bathroom floor, the head of Jamie's cock poking purply out from the waistband of his pyjama bottoms. Luz's nipples appropriately enough the shape and size of pencil erasers against Jamie's chest. Her hands tangled in his mane of hair.

Danny stands on shaky legs. "Thanks, guys," he says, covering himself with the towel again. They break apart. Barely.

"Thank you, Danny," says Luz, blinking up at him, her voice low as he has never heard it.

"Hope it helped," Jamie grunts, biting the inside of his cheeks, and Danny smiles, knowing that they are both doing everything they can not to fuck at his feet.

"It did," he says with a smile, and leaves, closing the door behind him.

• • •

Once Danny returns to his bed — cursing the fact that he's forgotten his pajamas — he realizes that it has helped. But it hasn't.

The randy insanity into which Danny was about to lose himself is gone — the edge of it taken off, at least — but as he settles naked between the sheets he finds himself hard as ever. Thinking about Suzie. And about what's just happened.

Has he betrayed Suzie? Or Jamie?

How would he feel if he saw Suzie sucking off a friend of theirs — Jamie? Bill? What did she do with Bill? She never wanted to discuss it, and Bill was always unwilling to talk specifics about what he got up to with Suzie — out of fear of pissing Danny off as much as out of delicacy, probably, since everyone knew how Danny felt about her, even before he did. Did she take Bill in her mouth? She jerked Danny off expertly enough — had she practiced on their friend? Or on Luke Harris, the jerk she'd dated briefly sophomore year? Had either of them buried his fingers or tongue or cock in her sweet folds? She told Danny she was still a virgin, but what did that mean?

And what about now? They've texted and — very carefully and infrequently — written since graduation, but Danny had pulled the Spiderman, Harry Potter routine, making made it very clear that, feel for her as he still did, they couldn't be together just now. She said she wouldn't give up on him. But he has no claim on her. And he's been away out of cell range and without internet for nearly two weeks.

Maybe she's seeing someone. Maybe she is fucking him right now.

Would watching that excite Danny as watching Luz clearly excited Jamie?

No.

No, he'd want to kill the guy, and then himself.

Not Suzie. No. He couldn't blame her; he gave her free rein.

He loves her. Fuck. He loves her.

But he'd rather die than watch some other boy's dick press through her lips, or her... lips.

And yet he's just come in Luz's mouth. Not Suzie's. How is that fair?

And here he is, hard as iron again, and Danny knows that he can't go back to Luz, that she and Jamie are busy — they must have gone back up to the bedroom; he can hear the bed above him beginning to move again — and that he has no right with anyone but Suzie (small breasts bouncing on either side of my face), but he has no right with her...

Her thin lips tracing the length of his cock as his tongue traces the line of her cunt lips...

Clear liquid is spilling from the tip of his cock and — in spite of himself — Danny uses his palm to spread the slick stuff along his penis and he feels a kind of panic sweeping over him. What the fuck's wrong with you, Danny? Can't you leave it alone?

Apparently not.

Circling the nub of flesh at the front of her, her clit, flicking it, making her squirm, feeling her swallow him to the root...

Suzie.

Danny's cock swells, pulsing in his hand; not soon, this round. He'll last for a long, long time, and hate himself from beginning to end.

The beast within him stretches, pleased at being given so much exercise, its wings spreading at the thought of those thin, pale lips against his, of her tongue — salty with his come — dancing with his own, and he begins to wail, knowing that he can rub himself bloody, can rub the fucking thing right off, but that still wouldn't satisfy his need, his hunger. "Oh, god, Suzie!"

"Danny?"

Danny's eyes fly open. There she is, in the doorway, face barely visible through her wild, red hair, shirt open, eyes wide and face flushed. "Danny? Are you all right?" she pants, staring at his cock as she walks the three feet to the bed. "What the fuck...?"

He leans up and his lips find her lips. His hands find her breasts — heaving, nipples diamond-hard.

"Here?" he groans into her mouth as he pulls the buttons off of the front of her shirt. He tastes her, breathes her in, stunned to find that all of his senses agree: Suzie is here. Still, he has to make sure. "Not hallucinating, you're really here?"

"Yup." She chuckles into his mouth and throws one leg across his bare waist. "Miss me, Danny?"

"Oh, fuck, Suzie, so much."

He can feel her lips smiling against his. Her hands find his bare ass and pull him to her until the head of his cock begins to press into the slick cleft that it has been straining to plow for months. She's not wearing panties.

"Wait. Wait. Suzie. Hold on," he mumbles into her mouth.

"Don't want to hold on. Want to fuck you."

"Suzie. Shit. Want you so much..."

"Want you too. Missed you. Want you so fucking much..." She mashes her slit along the shaft of his cock. "Don't want to fuck this? I'm on the Pill, have been for... Or... Want to stick that beautiful thing of yours in my backside, Danny? You can. I'm yours. My ass. My cunt. My mouth. My tits. Anything you want. All yours. But please, Danny," she urges, an edge of crazy desperation in her voice. "Fuck first, talk later. Or fuck and talk. But please...!"

He may be an idiot, but Danny di Angelo is not completely stupid. He spears up into her tight heat. "Fuck!" they both shout, and then, after a moment of stunned, still silence, they laugh and move, their pelvises finding a comfortable rhythm almost immediately. Danny feels her laughter around his cock, and that makes him happier than anything, happier even than the smooth, soft flesh that is clutching his penis.

They roll, and he can feel how deeply he's pushed into her tight, hot...

As much as being inside of Luz's mouth transcended his own ministrations, this outdoes that: body against body, her cunt tight and grasping around his thrusting cock, her breasts bouncing against his chest, mouth searching mouth and it's Suzie....

Luz. Fuck. He's gone from one girl to another before his dick has even had time to dry.

Pelvis still rocking against pelvis, he pushes back just enough to look down on her. Sees her, beautiful beyond words, eyes and mouth wide with wonder. "I love you so much, Suzie. I never said. I'm sorry." As if to give her the measure of his love, he withdraws his cock to the tip, almost to the point of losing contact, and then plunges it back in to her. Sheathing himself in her. Losing himself in her. And every ripple of her as he does is like some ridiculous, miraculous explosion; he feels like a never-ending Roman candle, flares and sparks of sensation connecting him to Suzie.

"Love you, too, Danny. It's okay." Her eyes fly wide as he thrusts back in again. "Fuck!"

They laugh again, but Danny feels a tinge of sadness coloring his joy. "Didn't hurt you, did I? Aren't girls...?" A thought passes through his head and he mentally tries to bat it away, banish it.

Her eyes glitter mischievously. "Not girls who've been riding for ten years, silly boy."

"Riding? Who've you been riding?" It's a joke. A tease. But it isn't, and he regrets it as soon as it leaves his mouth.

Her hands push back on his hips, stopping his thrusts. "Hey! They're a hell of a lot bigger than you, and they walk on four feet."

Suzie's bright brown eyes narrow and darken. "For that matter, boys are supposed to explode within the first thirty seconds, not bang away for ten minutes. Anyone been riding you while I've been serving pizza, pining away for you at home, di Angelo?"

"No!" Danny says, but his face falls, and she sees it and her chin juts out dangerously.

"What's going on, Danny?" she asks, twisting away from him so that they almost disengage.

"No, Suzie, stop. Please. Talk while fucking, right?" He kisses her and holds her tight. After a moment he feels her legs pull him back in.

"Okay," she sighs, her face still not quite open. "So what gives, Danny? What's turned you into Mr. Everlast?"

Sighing, Danny looks into her eyes, willing her to believe the truth. "I've been dying here, Suzie, thinking of you every day. Every night."

She peers at him, gauging his honesty. Slowly, she begins to rock against him again, and he groans. "Thinking about me, were you, Danny?"

"More than thinking, Suzie."

She grins, a hint of wariness flashing in her eyes. "Always said you were a jerk-off."

Now it is his turn to laugh. "Yeah, well, I pretty well earned that title lately."

She leans up and kisses his nipple. "Poor boy."

"But... Suzie..."

She looks at him, more trusting but nervous. Their movement together is small, now, but exquisite. The sparks all the brighter for being fewer.

"Tonight..."

"Tonight, what? You pick up some local girl to fill your lonely nights, Danny? Fucking some mermaid out on the lake? Sasquatch?"

"No, Suzie, no, it's not like that, I swear, I..."

A shudder passes through her. "Just tell me, Danny. You

fucked some girl —"

"What? No." They are belly to belly, resting, neither moving. This really isn't how Danny wanted his first time with Suzie — with anyone — to go.

"Two weeks, I've been sitting at home, or at the fucking pizzeria, missing you, nobody to talk to except Alice." Suzie's best friend aside from Danny and Luz, and very sweet, but probably the most boring girl on the face of the earth. "And I was lying in bed tonight and I thought, fuck it. Fuck it. Stole Mom's car, drove two hours with one hand on the wheel and the other in my crotch, and boom, here I was, ready for ravishing."

"You were in your bed?" Danny grins, beginning to slide into her again.

Her eyes get bright and cagey. "Didn't say it was *my* bed, now did I?"

The beast is back in Danny's chest, scaly and furious, as he thinks about her state when she arrived. Clothes undone. Face flushed. Cunt wet and ready. Nipples hard as pebbles. "No? Whose, then, Suzie?" Even after a two hour drive...

He is beginning to thrust harder, and she meets his thrusts, her hips slamming against his. "Jealous, Danny?"

Furious as he is, he is also ashamed. And feeling very, very good everywhere except inside of his head. And he owes her the truth, whatever she has been doing; he was the one who broke it off with her. As he is about to tell her about Luz, about Jamie's offer and Luz's mouth, there is a loud yelp from above the ceiling and a crash that shakes dust from the beams.

She blinks. "What the fucking hell was that?"

He can't help but grin. "Jamie. Luz. I think they just broke the bed."

She favors him with a red-cheeked smirk. "You're fucking joking."

Shaking his head, Danny laughs. "No, honest. They've been going at it so hard lately, I'm amazed it's lasted this long."

"So they finally managed it! Wasn't sure Luz'd have the balls.

Way to go...!"

He withdraws, and then plunges in deep once more.

"Can't blame them," Suzie says, shuddering again. "This feels pretty damned good."

"Yeah." Danny suddenly remembers the whip-like, rolling motion that Jamie had been employing in the living room. *I wonder...*

As his pubic bone bucks against her clit, Suzie's eyes open wide and she gasps. "OH! Fuck, Danny... Just... I don't care who you fucked, I really don't, but please don't ever do this with anyone else, okay?"

"Don't want to..." Amazingly, Danny can feel pressure building up behind his balls, the balls that are slapping against Suzie's ass. Time to confess and demand confession later. This is where he wants to be. "No one else. Ever. Never fucked anyone."

She is clawing at his back, the high, bubbling sigh in his ear signaling that she is as close as he is. "Me either, Danny. I swear. You're. Only. Boy. 'Ve ever. Fucked."

"Good!" he cries. And he is crying, his cock plunging into her, his heart opening out to her. "Couldn't stand it, Suzie. Kill me. If you..."

"Ah!" The bed is rocking against the wall, and Danny knows precisely how it would sound if he were on the floor below. If there were a floor below.

"Yours!" they both howl and orgasm overcomes them both and they collapse, tangled in each other irredeemably.

Some time later, Danny becomes aware again of time.

"I love you, Danny." Her voice sounds low and moist.

Danny's glasses seem to have flown off of his face. Sweat, tears and astigmatism make her a pink-and-orange blur. He leans to the center, knowing he'll find something to kiss. Her nose. "Love you, Suzie."

They lie there, each gasping for breath. Finally — finally — Danny's cock begins to soften, satisfied at last. He starts to withdraw, but she holds him close, arms and legs clasping.

"So," she says, her voice small, "who do I have to thank for getting you all... ready for me?"

He hides his face behind her ear. "Luz," he whispers.

"Luz!" she gasps. "Danny, how could you two do that to Jaime?"

"It was his idea."

"What?"

As he tells her — as he describes the whole evening, including the two early solo sessions, the cold shower, and their friends' solution — Suzie's grip on him begins both to tighten and to soften, and he realizes that she's now crying, she, who never cries. "Oh, Danny, you poor son of a bitch. I'm so sorry."

"Don't be," he murmurs, tasting the salt of her tears as he kisses her. "My fault. And... You're here now."

"I'm not going away, Danny. I won't leave you again. I won't."

Danny rests his forehead against hers. Can feel her heart beating against his chest. Around his cock. Being apart from her nearly drove him over the cliff. Can he stand to do that again? On the other hand, they're going to colleges three time zones apart. And everyone says long-distance relationships don't work. And high-school romances don't last. And... On the other hand... "Let's think about it. We'll talk about it tomorrow. I just... I know I can't think straight just now."

"Oh!" Suzie says and chuckles. "I have that effect on you, do I?"

"Yes. Your body is kind of amazing. And... You. You make it so that nothing else in the world is real. "

"Oh. I... Thank you, Danny."

"Thank me?"

She is crying again.

"It's okay, Suzie. Really. Come on. I love you."

The sound that escapes Suzie's mouth is a high, keening sigh, not unlike the sound she makes when she's about to come; but this time she sounds as if her heart is breaking, and he pulls her tight against him. He rolls on his back, her body still joined to his, her face still buried in his neck. For a long time, he rocks her there, kissing her, stroking her back.

Eventually, she stills, only hiccoughing occasionally. She leans back and sits up on him, his cock still planted limp inside of her. Her hair blazes against the dull white of the plaster ceiling, but her skin is so pale that he can barely tell where she begins and ends. Her eyes, though — those he can see, black smudges. And her mouth and nipples, bright in a sea of white and softer pink. "It's so amazing to see you without your glasses," she sighs. "Your eyes are so beautiful. So bottomless. You really can't see without them?"

He shakes his head.

"Oh. Well, it's probably just as well. Because... Danny, you've explained the state you were in tonight..."

A heavy weight suddenly settles into Danny's middle — and it's nothing to do with the light pressure of Suzie's pelvis against his. "Suzie, I told you. I don't blame you. I broke things off with you. You had every right to see any boy in town. I just — "

Her hands clutch at his shoulders. "Danny! Believe me, please! I haven't been seeing — or kissing, or boffing, or blowing, or touching — any fucking boys. I swear — "

"Thank god," Danny moans, reaching up to her face. "I'm not like Jamie, Suzie. The idea of another boy's hands on you... When Jamie and I saw you and Bill kissing at the junior prom, I wanted..." He takes a shaky breath. "I felt as if I had a fucking dragon inside of me trying to claw its way out and kill him. And that was before you and I ever... The idea of you with any other boy is more than I can stand, Suzie. I'm sorry. It's stupid."

"It's not stupid, Danny," Suzie says, touching his cheek. "It's the sweetest thing I've ever heard. But..."

"What, Suzie?" Dread settles into Danny's gut again. "Please just tell me so I don't have pictures of you and every boy in town in my head. Just tell me who."

"Please, Danny. Promise you won't be... Promise, no matter how upset you are, you'll forgive me."

He takes a deep breath. "I promise."

"What if..." She takes a slow, steadying breath. "Danny, what if it wasn't a boy?"

The monster is back inside of him, but it isn't cold or scaly; it's hot and chuckling. "What?" A grown man? No, Danny knows that's not what she means...

"Alice. Alice's the only friend that I could talk to about you, Danny, she's the only one I could really talk to, and she's your friend too, and she's been very... I was with her, tonight, and she was the one who said I should come... Um... She's been so... helpful."

Helpful. Like Luz.

Danny's cock twitches inside of Suzie and begins to grow.

"Oh!" she gasps.

Alice's wide mouth on Suzie's breasts. Her fingers circling Suzie's clit as Suzie calls out Danny's name. "Oh, god, Suzie..."

"Danny?" Suzie laughs, relieved. She begins to move up and down on his incredibly-erect-once-again penis, her skirt splashing against Danny's belly. "Fuck, Danny. Guess you didn't mind too much." Alice's tongue running along Suzie's open, wet lips. Pressing her fingers gently into Suzie while Suzie pinches at her nipples... just as she is doing now. Alice's white ass high in the air...

He begins to thrust up into her — fluid from their first fuck flowing down — and Suzie moves against him. "Feels so... Fuck! You're an over-the-top, twisted fucker after all, aren't you, Danny-boy?"

"You have no idea," grunts Danny. "I have no idea. But let's find out."

# The Trouble with Triplets, pt. I

## A Cautionary Tale —

### A sneak peek at the beginning of a new threesome story!

**K.D. West:** *This is part of one of my* Erotic Tales/Love Letters *stories. In these stories, Ken is writing his young lover (and former student) Allison while she's away at college, sharing the stories of his adventures as a young man.* When he writes this letter, she has been teasing him with the idea of a threesome between Allison, Ken, and Allison's BFF and sometime innamorata Jordan. Here's the beginning of Ken's response; it doesn't go in quite the direction that Ken expected, but I think he found the ending... satisfying.*

I've participated — or almost participated — in three threesomes, only one of which was actually my idea.

Not one of them turned out the way any of us expected.

The first two were both ideas of Cindy's, which shouldn't have been a surprise, though it was at the time.

The summer that I first met her, we were playing Viola and Sebastian in a local production of Twelfth Night.

That summer was the first time that I fell in love. Oh, I loved Dana. I still do. But with Cindy it was if the color leached out of everything else in the room when she walked in.

The problem was, I wasn't the only one in the cast following her around like a duckling. One of the other guys in the cast, Michael, who was playing Antonio, rarely left her elbow. He and I got along well, we hung out together during the show and after.

About a week after the show opened, we were at a local bar — I was underage, but no one ever asked. As had become our habit, Cindy, Michael and I had split off from the rest of the cast, and were hanging at a table at the back of the bar, trading stories about nothing in particular. "I have to tinkle," said Cindy, standing. "Don't talk about me took much."

Once she had gone, Michael turned to me and said, "You okay with me going after Cindy?"

I swigged my beer, thought about it for a moment. "Not sure. You okay if I went after her?"

A rueful smile on his face, Michael shook his head and raised his bottle. "Best man wins?"

I clicked my beer to his. "Best man wins."

When Cindy sauntered back from the bathroom, I was still trying to come up with a first move in the chess game, but Michael beat me to it. "Hey, Cindy, a friend of mine over at River Shakes — " A Shakespeare festival just over the mountain from ours. " — just offered me a couple of comps to tomorrow's show of their Twelfth Night. Want to come?"

I gawked at him, at his audacity at getting off the mark so quickly.

He shot me a wink.

Cindy sounded thrilled. "That'd be great! Jen, who's playing their Viola, is an old friend of mine." The first woman Cindy had ever fallen in love with — but I wouldn't find out about that until much later. Cindy reached out and grabbed my wrist. "You want to come too, Ken?" Turning back to Michael, she smiled. "I don't suppose your friend could manage another comp?"

Michael flashed me a look of what I hoped was mock annoyance and raised his bottle. "No problem."

I laughed and tapped his bottle once more with mine. Quoting from one of our scenes together, I said, "I can no other answer give than thanks!"

Michael grunted, but smiled back, and Cindy laughed her low, throaty laugh.

I was driving my dad's beat up old Triumph that summer, and so we all jumped in and rode over the treacherous road to River Shakes the next night and enjoyed the hell out of watching other peoples' takes on the roles that we were performing. While Cindy told her friend Jen very breathily how wonderful her performance had been, Michael and I chatted with our counterparts — Michael's part in their show had been played by a woman: Antonia. We laughed about the evident sexual tension between Antonio/a and Sebastian. Michael told them that our nickname for the character had been the Swishbuckler.

Michael and his counterpart were actually getting along well — really well. She was flirting with him like all hell. (The other Sebastian flirted with me for about thirty seconds before smiling at me, giving me a wink, and turning off the full-press charm. I've always had that affect on gay men.)

When Antonia started putting her hand on my friend's shoulder, I decided to see if I could press my advantage — and do him a favor at the same time. "Michael, Cindy and I have rehearsal for Cyrano tomorrow morning, we should get back."

As I'd hoped and expected, the Antonia said, "Oh, if you don't have rehearsal, Michael, I'm sure we could find someplace for you to spend the night." Her tone made it very clear that the someplace would be very warm and cozy.

Michael's jaw worked, and he looked over at me as if to say, Damn! How'd you manage that? "Uh, thanks, but I should get back too." He squeezed the woman's hand. "Maybe later in the run?"

She grinned. "Maybe."

"Hey, Cindy," Michael said, "you ready to head back? You and this prick have rehearsal tomorrow morning."

Cindy pouted, gave her friend a kiss on the cheek, and then pulled the two of us out toward where I'd parked the Triumph.

"Bye!" called the Antonia. The other Sebastian and I both laughed.

On the ride back, Cindy sat in the back and talked about the production we'd seen, both its strengths (Jen's Viola, in her mind) and its weaknesses (everything else).

Grinning, I looked over at Michael and said, "Actually, I thought the Antonia was great."

"Yes," granted Cindy, almost grudgingly. "She was pretty good."

"And she thought our Antonio was damned cute."

I thought for a moment that Michael was going to punch me. Good thing that I was at the wheel on a windy road.

"Well," said Cindy, throwing an arm around Michael's neck, "he is!"

Michael smiled smugly at me.

Then Cindy kissed me on the cheek. "And our Sebastian is much hunkier than theirs."

I smirked back at Michael.

We chatted and flirted through the rest of the drive.

We reached Cindy's place first — a house that the theater had found for her to house-sit. "It's not even midnight," she said. "Come on up and take a hot tub with me."

Michael and I looked at each other, both a little shocked by the invitation, and each unwilling to back down. "Sure," we both said.

While we waited for the tub to heat up, we drank beers and chatted. Well, Michael and I were both feeling a bit uncertain, so mostly Cindy talked. But she was very comfortable with that.

After a half hour, steam was rising off of the bubbling water. "Why don't you boys jump in," Cindy said as coquettishly as her husky contralto could manage. "I'll be right out."

Once she'd left the deck, Michael stripped down to his boxers. When I jumped into the hot tub commando, however, he pulled off the shorts with a look of grim determination.

We were so aware of each other that neither of us noticed Cindy stepping into the tub behind us. "Hi, boys."

We turned around. She was naked. The moonlight turned her saffron skin to bronze. Her brown nipples shown dark and her public bush was a stark, shining black.

I don't know about Michael, but I was fully erect before she had gotten all of the way in. I was overjoyed that I had sat already.

We sat there, equidistant in that round hot tub, not quite out of touching distance from each other, and talked quietly some more about the production that we'd seen that night. About the Cyrano we were rehearsing.

Cindy's small breasts floated on the water, the thick nipples poking through the foam.

When the talk finally ran silent, Cindy sat up on the edge of the tub, moonlight burnishing her glistening skin. "You guys find me... attractive. Don't you?"

Michael and looked at each other, nodded, and then looked away.

"Well," Cindy continued, voice low and throaty, "you are both very attractive too. And so here is my proposal: I want to fuck you both. At the same time."

I could hear Michael cough in shock, even as her suggestion, which shouldn't have been a surprise but for some reason was, made my jaw drop.

Grinning at our reactions, Cindy continued, "But only if it's both of you. If either or both of you are uncomfortable with this, and want to leave, I'll totally understand, and that we'll be the last time we'll ever talk about it, but I'll expect the other one to leave as well."

We sat there for a good thirty seconds, listening to the water and the bubbles.

I looked over at Michael. "I'm game," I said, though I was sure that I didn't know what I was agreeing to.

Michael looked at me, then at Cindy, and then back at me. He stood. His cock was half-mast in the hot water. "I can't," he whispered.

"Michael," said Cindy, but he was already out of the tub, off the deck, and out of the house.

I've always wondered if he bothered to get dressed on his half-mile walk back to his place.

I looked back at Cindy, who hadn't moved, whose flesh seemed to be blossoming with goosepimples. "Cindy," I said, "please — "

She shook her head. "No, Ken, I meant it, I can't fuck just one of you, I — "

"How about I don't fuck you?" I whined. "How about I just eat you?"

Cindy didn't say yes. She didn't say no. Her face was wide and uncertain, but her legs parted and I took that for my answer.

That set up a pattern that lasted through the rest of that summer. We never fucked, but whenever Cindy was feeling horny, she would spread her legs, or lift her skirt — or, once, during the interminable last act of Cyrano, her nun's habit — and, like the lapdog that I'd become, I would pleasure her with my mouth.

I know that I must have gotten off somehow during these exchanges, though I'm pretty sure it was by my own hand most of the time.

Michael and Cindy and I stopped hanging out all of the time. The Antonia from River Shakes started appearing during their dark nights. "The best man won," I toasted him.

He grinned and nodded to where Cindy was talking with her friend Jen and with Antonia — whose actual name was Sally. "You and Cindy?" he asked.

I shook my head.

That night, Cindy took me back to her hot tub again — and as I brought her off, she moaned out the name Jen.

When I asked her about that, Cindy blanched. Tearfully, she admitted that she was in love with her strawberry blonde friend, and had been for a while.

"I like guys too," she said, searching my face.

"I don't really care who you like," I said, "if you don't love me."

"I'm sorry, Ken. I do like you." Reaching between us, she grabbed my cock. "You want to fuck me, tonight?"

It wasn't much of a fuck. And it didn't change how she felt about me. But I'd be lying if I said I didn't feel much happier afterward.

*Allison's stories are told in the Juliet Takes Flight tales. And yes: there will be a FFM ménage story coming in that series soon!*

Dear Reader,

Thanks so much for reading this collection of stories featuring groups of friends becoming... **much** more than friendly! I have more that I'll be sharing — so I'd love to know what you think!

See below for more of my stories — including a sneak preview of a sexy MMF ménage story from my collaboration with the wonderful Mary Cyn, *Wedding Belles: Steamy Wedding Stories*.

I write these stories because I really enjoy telling them, both the sexy and the not-so-sexy bits. If you've gotten this far, I hope that you've enjoyed reading it too. Either way, I'd love to hear from you. If you want to talk to me about my stories — if you have comments or questions or just want to grumble or gush — wow, I would sure love to hear what you have to say!

You can email me at **kdwest@stillpointdigital.com**, or you can go to my blog (**kdwestwrites.wordpress.com**) and send me a comment.

You can also connect with me on Twitter (@**KDWestWrites**), Facebook, Pinterest, Google+, Tumblr, or even LinkedIn. If you let me know that you've read this note, I'll send you a short story for free by way of thanks. I really look forward to hearing from you.

Whatever you thought of these pieces, I'd also really love it if you would review this book — or any of the stories — wherever you share your opinions about what you read. Reviews help readers, and they help writers too! We need to know what you liked (and even what you didn't)

There are more stories coming out in this series; I'm coming out with a new one every month. Keep an eye on my blog or on the Stillpoint/Eros site for news

Until next time!

*K. D. West*

# Also by K. D. West
## print books, ebooks and audiobooks:

### Collections:
Four Erotic Tales: Letters to Allison (M/F)
Juliet Takes First (M/F, F/F)
Three for Three: A Trio of Friendly MMF Ménage Tales... Plus!
(M/M/F, M/F/M, M/F)
The Visitor Arrives (M/M/F)
The Visitor & Other Threesomes
(M/M/F, M/F/M, M/F)
Wild West: Collected Erotic Tales, volume I
(M/F, F/F, M/M/F)

### COMING SOON!
The Visitor Entertains (F/M/M)
The Visitor Takes a Trip (F/M/M)
The Visitor Has Company (F/M/M, F/F/M)
Meredith (M/F)
Allison (M/F, M/F/F)
Juliet Takes the Floor (M/F/F)
Juliet Takes Charge (M/F, F/F, M/F/F)
Opening the Door (M/F, M/F/F)
The Trouble with Triplets (M/M/F, M/F/F)

(Go to the next page to get a sneak peek at the next story in this series!

# Plus One

A sneak preview at a story nuptial threesome naughtiness
by Mary Cyn
from *Wedding Belles: Steamy Wedding Stories!*

We keep talking through dinner and I manage to forget his eyes, his lips, those incredible shoulders. I manage to tear my eyes away from him and have an actual conversation, not just drooling and *Night Court* quotes. Which is good, because he's really fun. He's hard to read, though. He's not just talking to me, which could indicate interest in me. And he's not just talking to Wyatt, which would almost definitely indicate interest in me. Unless he's gay. I don't get that sense, but you never know. But he's talking to us, not just making small talk with the whole table. So I don't know what that means. Maybe nothing.

Toasts happen and then we all settle into our entrees, that awkward silence descending on the table. We've all introduced ourselves, said how we know the bride and groom. And now we're just a bunch of not-quite-strangers eating awkwardly.

Till Dan takes action. "Ok, Wedding Table Icebreaker," he announces. "Is a hot dog a sandwich?"

The table is quiet for a second, but it's a quizzical silence, and it only lasts a second.

"No," says Wyatt. "Of course not. It's a hot dog. It has a different name."

"Ah," says Dan, "but so do hamburgers and they are often listed in the sandwich section of a menu."

"And sandwiches have names, too," I add. "Like a Reuben or a cheesesteak or a hoagie or grinder or whatever."

"Good point," says the person across from me.

"And," I add, catching on to the game, "what is a hot dog, if not meat between two pieces of bread? That is a sandwich."

"But it's a special kind of bread," says the girl next to Wyatt. And suddenly the whole table is in on the debate. Dan smiles at me.

"Well done, sir." I toast him.

"It's the perfect ice breaker," he tells me. "There's enough points to get everyone talking but the subject is far too dumb for anyone to get angry about. Unless they're, like, a superdouche."

"But who wants to talk to them anyway?"

"Exactly." His smile lingers on me a moment too long and I feel that excited little shiver in my body.

• • •

After dinner he asks me to dance.

"Assuming you don't mind?" he says deferentially to Wyatt.

"Not at all." Wyatt smiles and stands. "There's a young lady I've been making eyes at. Best to follow through."

"Godspeed, sir." Dan takes my hand as we go to the dance floor. I try not to look like I'm at my junior prom, even though that's how I feel. Or that's how I think I would have felt if a really hot guy had danced with me at my junior prom. "So, what's the actual deal with you and, uh…"

He does like me! Forgetting the name of the perceived competition is a dead giveaway.

"I'm his wingman date," I admit.

"Ooh, bad choice." He shakes his head. "Any girl who sees him with you is going to stay far away. Unless she thinks way too much of herself. You're way too attractive, there's far too much chemistry between you two. You read as a couple. You, my dear, are a cock block date."

"I… Thank you? I guess?"

He laughs, a little embarrassed. "Sorry," He blushes a little. "I overthink things."

"Not a problem." Damn, time to be honest. "I guess, I'm not just his wingman. I'm also his consolation sex." Oh, god. That sounds terrible now.

I see his eyebrows go up in disbelief.

"No, it's not…" I try to correct myself. "We're friends. Friends who have sex sometimes. And, well, he and Emily used to go out and… I don't think he wants to go home alone. So, if he doesn't find someone…"

"He gets to go home with you?" Dan smirks. "Don't you worry you're taking away his motivation?"

I laugh. "I thought men were motivated by conquests."

"Those are fun," he concedes. "But, let's be honest, the first time you have sex with someone is usually the worst."

"Not always."

"No, not always. Some people, your hands just know where to go." I'm suddenly extra aware of his hand in the small of my back. "But even then it's usually better with someone you know. That's when you get to do the weird stuff."

I laugh even harder this time. Christ, I hope I'm not blushing again. "How'd you know I like the weird stuff?" I giggle.

"Wishful thinking," he murmurs.

Damn. I really like this guy. I pull him closer to me.

"You know," he says over my shoulder, "If Wyatt's young lady isn't receptive, he might have to share you with me."

I look at him, not sure if I'm more shocked by his forwardness or the fact that he just made the same joke that Wyatt had.

"I mean —" He looks alarmed, worried he's misjudged my interest. "— if you're amenable, of course."

"You have no idea just how amenable I would be." My shock melts to a smile. "I was just surprised that you and Wyatt expressed such similar thoughts."

"Did we?" It's his turn to be shocked. "I didn't think… He doesn't seem the type."

"Oh, Wyatt will surprise you. It's not all Southern charm."

"And what about you?" he asks. "Will you surprise me?"

"Man, I hope so."

This shouldn't be romantic, should it? I mean, there's no mystery. We know we want to fuck. There's no chase, no seduction but… I find myself incredibly charmed. All he has to do is dip me and I feel dizzy with romance. Maybe it's the champagne or my weakness for formal wear, but I really like this guy. And the fact that he's willing, hell, proposing to have a threesome with me and Wyatt… It's like finding a unicorn.

We sit back down and talk till Wyatt returns to our table.

"Where's the young lady?" Dan asks.

"Boyfriend at home," sighs Wyatt, a little wistful but not too glum.

"Tragic!" says Dan. "Who wouldn't want to sleep with you?"

They talk like they're old friends. There's no territorial vibe from either one, which is kind of amazing. I've dated a lot of jealous guys and I know I'm supposed to find it flattering or whatever but for me it's just annoying. There is no greater boner-killer than some guy bristling at the thought of another man wanting me. If you're going to date a hot chick, you should be prepared for the fact that other people will find her hot. I mean, duh. Isn't that part of the point?

But it's not like that tonight. We drink together. We tell stories. They take turns dancing with me. We all dance together to the fast songs. As we get drunker, Wyatt tells the story of how we met at a bachelor party and then prompts me to tell Dan about my ideal wedding. I'm drunk enough to tell him. The whole messy, pervy story. And he seems… charmed. A lot of guys are shocked, or shift uncomfortably, or ask why the girls can't be involved in the circle jerk at the end. But he just smiles his warm, inviting smile, his eyes sparkling to remind me just how blue they are.

The night is winding down and we're all very pleasantly drunk. Our hands make affectionate little contacts; my nail sliding up the side of Wyatt's leg, Dan's fingertips brushing my shoulders, my palms caressing both their knees. The conversation slows down and there's that pervasive stillness of something important unsaid.

"I'll say this," Wyatt proclaims, a little unsteady, "Every time Emily looks over here, she seems more and more confused."

We all laugh.

"I'm not surprised," I say. "Emily assumes that I sleep with every guy she sees me talk to more than twenty minutes."

"Wait, you don't?" says Dan in mock indigence. "I have been lead grossly astray!"

We all laugh again and we suddenly seem very close, physically close. Like someone surreptitiously shoved our chairs together. There's that stillness again. Wyatt breaks it.

"So what do you say, Dan?" He puts an arm around me. "You want to be our plus-one?"

I look at Dan, hoping my eyebrows are poised at a cocky and seductive angle. Dan smiles again, downs the last of his champagne and says, "I do."

## Plus One: Kat McKinney Wedding Slut, Part II
from
*Wedding Belles: Steamy Wedding Stories*
by K.D. West and Mary Cyn

# About K.D. West

The author of the Erotic Tales: Letters to Allison and Juliet Takes
Flight story cycles as well as the up-coming novel A Joy Forever: An
Erotic Education, K.D. West is a teacher, writer and performer living
in a small suburb of a big city:

> Not a huge amount to say — I'm an author of steamy stories who
> happens to be a teacher; these things don't mix well in public, so I
> tend to be fairly quiet about real life in my blogging. I am, however,
> interested in all sorts of things -- books, writing, theater, mythology,
> and, obviously, erotica! I'm a huge reader of genre fiction — mostly
> mysteries and fantasy, but also science fiction and historical romance.

West has written two intertwined series involving a young woman and
her older lover (the *Juliet Takes Flight* and *Erotic Tales: Letters to Allison*
stories) and a series of stories about friends discovering that they can
become much more *(Friendly Ménage Tales)*. Also on the way: an erotic
paranormal/urban fantasy novel involving a long lost friend coming
all-but-literally back from the dead, and showing a happily married
couple just what they'd been missing.

# Stillpoint Digital Press

Stillpoint Digital Press creates fine ebook, audiobook, and print editions in genres from fiction to literary nonfiction, from memoir to poetry.

In addition to publishing, Stillpoint provides editing and other publishing services to independent publishers, aiming to give a human face to digital publishing, offering a full range of editorial services, from editing, layout and ebook conversion to distribution and marketing.

For more about Stillpoint Digital Press and its books and services, visit us on the web at http://stillpointdigitalpress.com

## READ MORE STILLPOINT TITLES:

### STILLPOINT/ROMANCE
*The Mercenary Major: A Regency Romance* by Kate Moore
*Sweet Bargain: A Regency Romance* by Kate Moore
*Sexy Lexy: A Contemporary Romance* by Kate Moore

### STILLPOINT/MYSTERY
*Death in a Fair Place: A Ben Felkin Mystery* by W.L. Taylor
*Dread in a Fair Place: A Ben Felkin Mystery* by W.L. Taylor

### STILLPOINT/THOUGHT
*Myths to Live By* by Joseph Campbell
*A Joseph Campbell Companion: Reflections on the Art of Living*
by Joseph Campbell
*Gods & Games: Toward a New Theology of Play* by David L. Miller
*Excursions to the Far Side of the Mind: A Book of Memes* by Howard Rheingold

### STILLPOINT/VERSE
*Easing into Dark* by Jaqueline Kudler
*Sacred Precinct* by Jaqueline Kudler
*Practice* by Dan Belmm
*Space/Gap/Interval/Distance* by Judy Halebsky
*The Stranger Dissolves* by Christina Downing

### STILLPOINT/MEMORY
*Sail Away: Journeys of a Merchant Seaman* by Jack Beritzhoff
*Pasta in My Bra: a Saga of Cerebral Palsy* by Nicole Sykes

AND MORE!
*stillpointdigitalpress.com*

# About Stillpoint/Eros

*Erotica to feed the mind, the spirit…*

*and, oh, yes, the body.*

*Fine erotica for the discerning individual,*

*available as ebooks, print books, and audiobooks!*

## Stillpoint/Eros

StillpointEros.com
@StillpointEros • facebook.com/StillpointEros
plus.google.com/StillpointErosBooks

# THE LAW & THE HEART
## STORIES TO BEND THE MIND & SOUL
# KENNETH SCHNEYER

Debut collection from Nebula-nominated author Kenneth Schneyer

*First, the law.* A time traveler confronts a judge to prevent four years of war. An author undergoes suspended animation to preserve his copyrights and escape his creditors. *Then, the heart.* A medical accident robs a husband of 20 years of marriage. A soldier mother struggles to tell the difference between her daughter and the alien enemy.

Exploring the seams where humanity and technology, society and individuality intersect, Schneyer presents thirteen mind-bending, thought-provoking tales of near and far futures that will amuse, amaze, and unsettle. The law will change, and the heart will change, and the heart will change the law. These stories confront the question of just what makes and keeps us human.

Includes four new, previously unpublished stories: "Grapple with Thee," "Half a Degree," "Exceptionalism," and "The Orpheus Fountain."

*The stories here are formally ingenious, even startling, and at the same time full of heart; the combination is brilliant and delightful. More please!* — **Kim Stanley Robinson**

*Schneyer extrapolates the future of our legal systems with the dexterity of an Asimov putting his robots through their paces and yet in these (lucky) thirteen stories you will meet people just like you who live lives you would never have imagined.* — **James Patrick Kelley**

**Stillpoint Digital Press**
stillpointdigital.com